PART ONE

GIRL Departs THREE

SPOKEN FOR SERIES

BOOK THREE

SUZIE T. ROOS

GIRL DEPARTS THREE, PART 1

Copyright © 2010, 2015, 2022 by Suzie T. Roos

Cover Design K Keeton Designs
Interior format by The Killion Group
http://thekilliongroupinc.com

DEDICATION

To my family & friends: Your loyalty and support means more than you can imagine. The countless hours you listen to me plot, rehash, act out, brainstorm and more, has been vital to the completion of these books.

When you are loved and respected, you can do *anything*!

CHAPTER 1

Tatum

Monday, January 1, 1990

THE BLAZING SUN ON MY tender eyes woke me. Muffled voices coming from inside the house made sure I was awake.

Nigel was lying next to me, still sleeping. His back was to me, exposing his muscular shoulders, reminding me how lucky I was. Waking up to the New Year with that view was something I could get used to.

I carefully got out of bed and made my way to the bathroom. It was ten in the morning and while I'd gotten a decent amount of beauty rest, last night's New Year's Eve Party had taken its toll and I wanted to freshen up.

When I came out, Nigel was sitting up in bed, watching TV. "Morning, Tate. How did you sleep?"

"Good. The bed is comfortable. How about you?"

"I always sleep well in this house."

After Nigel took his turn in the bathroom, we put the bedroom back together.

"Nige, what can I do out there to help clean up

from the party?"

"Nothing. Between Lester, my mom, and Bren, we can take care of everything. Sometimes Jessie and Tommy stay to help."

"If you're sure . . . though I really don't mind cleaning."

"Nope. No need. There's more than enough hands on deck." Nigel stepped up to me and held my upper arms. Feeling his hands on my skin in the morning was another thing I could get used to. "Thanks for staying the night. I hope you had a good time."

"I did . . . you told me you loved me. Nothing is better than that."

Nigel pulled me against his chest. "I love you so much. You drive me insane."

"Well, the same goes for me too." I popped up on my tiptoes and gave him a tender kiss.

"You're the best start a guy could have to the New Year." Nigel carried my duffle bag out to the garage door. He said goodbye to other friends who were leaving while I found Andi and Di. They were finishing up in the bedroom they'd stayed in.

I leaned against the doorframe, facing them. "I'm gonna be leaving soon. How 'bout you cats?"

They shoved the last bit in their bags and zipped up. With her bag in hand, Andi walked over to me. "Tate, I have a big favor to ask you."

Di glared at me from behind Andi. That was not a good sign.

"What is it?"

"Go to the airport with us, with me?"

"Airport? For what?"

"Hear me out. Matt is landing in a couple of hours.

I've never even met his mom and dad before—"

"Nope. No can do. Sorry."

"Tatum." Andi grabbed my wrist. I glared at her, and she immediately released her hold. "Please? Look, you don't even have to say anything to them. They don't have to know you're even there. We . . . we can . . . go to the exit terminal. The big one before baggage claim. You can sit off to the side there. Di's coming."

Di walked past us. "Yeah, you talked me into driving your ass."

I watched Di carry her bag out into the kitchen.

"Tatum, I beg you. Please?"

"Why?"

"You wanna know why?"

"Did you not hear me?"

"Tatum, you're not afraid of things. You deal with them. When you're with me, I can do things I wouldn't normally be able to do without you there."

I stood up all the way. "I'm not your mom. And I'm afraid of everything." After all the years we'd been friends, Andi still didn't know me. What she thought was my bravery was a front, because it was easier that way than dealing with the reality of shitty things happening in my life.

"You? No, you're not."

Nigel walked up to us. "What's going on?"

"My boyfriend, Matt, is coming back home in a couple of hours," Andi said. "I'm trying to get Tate to go to the airport with me."

"You don't want to go?" Nigel asked.

If only he understood what he was asking. I couldn't tell him who Matt's cousin was. Nigel would never let me near Andi alone again. Nigel and I had such a wonderful time together, why ruin it? "Not particularly."

"Mom just got here with bagels and pastries. Whatever you decide, come eat first. I can still drive you home if you don't go with Andi."

Nigel walked back into the kitchen.

"Andi, don't. You know I can't tell him who Matt's cousin is. Don't use Nigel as a pawn."

"Sorry, you're right. But I still want you to go with me. Otherwise I won't be able to see Matt until school on Tuesday. Look, it's not like *he'll* be there."

"I don't care to see *any* Bertano, whether Zach would be there or not. You can see Matt tomorrow, Andi. You can't possibly understand how it will affect me seeing any of his family. What if his parents are there? I can't take that chance."

Of course, I couldn't let her know the night before I'd overheard her telling Di that Zach had slept with Mariacella, the Italian girl his Gramps was forcing him to marry. Not only that, but he had slept around a lot since they'd forced him to live in Italy. Zach clearly did not care about me anymore, let alone love me. Not one phone call since he'd up and left me after Thanksgiving. No Christmas card. No message from his cousins. Nothing. I didn't want to go anywhere near the Bertano family. Zach didn't exist to me anymore.

"Andi, I can't." I walked toward the kitchen.

She followed me. "Please, Tatum. I'm scared."

I spun around, and she nearly ran into me. "Give me one good reason why. And being scared is no reason to inconvenience me."

I noticed we had an audience in the kitchen. Jessie, Di, Nigel, Bren, and Anna stood on high alert, watching me.

I lowered my head and voice. "Not here."

"Tate, what's the big deal? Just go with her, hon," Nigel said.

If only my death glare made Andi leave me alone—but it didn't. She was putting me in a very uncomfortable situation. Di stepped up and placed her hand on my shoulder. "I'll be there. We'll stay off to the side. If I don't drive her there, she can't see him. Sounds like he has to do a family dinner when they get back, and she'll go with them. But you and I can leave as soon as she meets up with Matt."

I took a deep breath, looking like psycho of the year in front of everyone.

Andi whispered. "I will owe you big time. Just go. You can leave when Matt gets there."

"You owe me big time, Andi."

Andi threw her arms around my neck. "Thank you. Thank you so much, Tate."

Someone needed to receive the sucker of the year award.

We ate breakfast and the three of us headed out. Nigel walked me out to Di's car. I leaned against the VW Rabbit. "We're going over to Grandpa Oscar's to make dinner with him for the New Year. I'll come by later tonight. Love you, m'lady."

"Sounds good. Tell Grandpa Oscar I said Happy New Year."

"Will do." Nigel gave me a goodbye kiss that made me forget the cold.

Di warmed the car and Andi jumped in the backseat, letting me take the front.

I got in and Nigel closed the door for me. "Drive safe. Talk tonight."

"You too. Love you."

Nigel rolled his eyes up, tucking his lips in—his signature action when he was wanted to kiss me, but couldn't. He blinked real fast and waved. "Bye, m'lady."

Di backed out of the driveway.

I rolled down the window and blew kisses at him. "Miss you already."

Di took her time driving away from Nigel's house. "You love him? Oh my gosh, Tate. That's awesome."

From the backseat, Andi reached up and patted my shoulder. "I'm so happy for you. Nigel's the best."

"He is. We had a great time before we went to bed last night."

"We heard the Jacuzzi going. I bet you had a good time." Di snickered.

"Believe it or not . . . we soaked in the tub filled with bubbles and just talked."

"Not," Andi shouted out, and laughed.

Di thought it was funny too.

"Well, we did. Now . . . not for long." They both chuckled. "But we did. I was kind of upfront with him about not wanting to have sex. We agreed it was too easy to last night, we would wait and let the tension build."

"Oh, you didn't?" Di said.

"What does that mean?"

"Do you know what it's like for a guy 'building tension,' forcing himself to not have sex?"

"Well, I'm sure like for us, it's not easy. I just want

to wait."

"You're scared he'll leave you like Zach did. I don't blame you, though."

"I am *not afraid* Nigel will leave me, Diane," I said with firm intention.

Andi scooted up to my seat and patted my shoulder. "Tate, she might be right. I know it's not what you want to hear, but if Zach didn't leave when he did, how much longer would you have made him wait? Now, with him gone, you're even more relieved you didn't sleep with him."

"Okay, forget I said anything at all. I'm not talking about my *relations* with you guys anymore."

Andi patted my shoulder again and they both dropped it, which was for the best since I'd gotten worked up. I didn't want to take my frustration out on my girlfriends because of how Zach had left me. They didn't deserve that.

Di turned on Lindbergh, one exit away from the airport. A short few minutes later and we pulled into the main terminal parking garage. I hoped Andi was going to pay for parking there, since it was expensive. Maybe her rich boyfriend would give her money. Especially, since he'd begged her to meet him at the airport.

From the garage, we walked in the level marked "baggage claim."

The big ramp to baggage claim was in front of us. On the left, luggage spilled onto the belts, circling until someone claimed them.

Up a ramp were some benches against the wall. I sat on one at the end.

"Andi, you go ahead. I'll wait here." Below ground

level, the baggage claim area was on the dim side. Skylights provided some light but today was cloudy. I stared at the *Spirit of St. Louis*, Charles Lindbergh's plane, hanging from the rafters.

Di sat beside me. "Yeah, Andi. As soon as Matt shows, we'll take off."

Andi headed up the ramp. "Thanks again for coming. I do appreciate it."

"Sure. Just remember you owe me one. I'll let you know what it is when I come up with something good."

Di swatted my shoulder. "Tate, stop. Go ahead, Andi. We'll wait here."

The speakers clicked on. "Flight two seventy-four from LaGuardia arriving at gate seven." The message repeated a second time.

"That could be them," Di said.

Andi gave us a bright smile and a thumbs-up. I supposed that was their flight number.

I got comfy and rested my head on the wall. "I'm tired all of a sudden."

"Are you sure you got any sleep last night?"

I turned my head to look at her. "I did. But not the eight hours I require. It's stupid, but if I don't get at least eight hours, I'll yawn all day."

"You should take Vitamin B12."

"What does that do?"

"It helps your energy. Just try it, it can't hurt. It's a B vitamin."

"Hmm, I'll have to look into it." I rolled my head back and closed my eyes.

"Flight two seventy-four is arriving at gate seven. Luggage claim M-three."

I supposed they were coming. Good. I wanted to get home to take a nap.

We heard a bunch of voices with accents. Di and I popped up and, sure enough, a group of Italians were making their way down the ramp. Andi kept looking around bodies. Maybe it was another family. The Bertanos weren't the only Italians.

"Matt?" Andi screeched.

Di and I popped up, startled. "Jesus, did she have to scream it?" I said.

Matt dropped his bag and ran for Andi, lifting her in the air and spinning her around. He kissed all over her face. It was sweet how much he had clearly missed her. I was happy for her.

A middle-aged couple walked up to them and stood. The guy, who was as big as Andre the Giant, said, "Matt? Is this your Andi?"

"Yeah, this is Andi. Andi, this is my mom and dad."

They exchanged pleasantries. Matt's mom grabbed Andi and hugged her, welcoming her to the family.

"Jesus, Di . . . look at how big that guy is."

"Well, now we know where Matt gets it from."

"Yeah." I laughed. "No joke. I'm ready to go. You?"

"Yeah, he's here now. Let's take off," Di said.

We grabbed our purses, got up, and headed toward the parking garage.

"Hey . . . you made it. Who drove you here?" Matt said.

I could just hear him.

"Di and Tatum did. Bye, guys. Thanks again," Andi called out.

Di and I waved, but kept going. I didn't want to have to talk to any of them. And I wasn't meeting anyone, not today.

"Matt? You okay?" Andi asked.

"Shit. Why is Tatum here?"

I refrained from flipping Matt off, although I really wanted to.

"What the hell is his problem?" Di whispered.

"No clue."

"That's Tatum? Damn it, not here," we heard Matt's father say.

That did it. I stopped. Di followed my lead. We both turned around to see what their problem was.

The moment I looked up the ramp, I saw him standing there, frozen, his bag at his side.

Zach.

CHAPTER 2

Tatum

I COULDN'T BELIEVE MY EYES. ZACH stood there, up the ramp, looking as if he couldn't believe what he was seeing either. That made two of us. He was wearing a baseball cap, shadowing his face. I had never seen him wear one before. Zach was wearing a nice new leather jacket. Thank the Lord it didn't scream, *I'm an Italian Mobster,* though. Which was good, but then again, what did I care?

I didn't wait for any more thoughts. I turned around and ran for the garage door. "Di, hurry. Get the car."

Up the ramp, you could hear random chatter and cussing from his family, but Zach didn't say anything. The sound of something being dropped echoed in the corridor. I glanced back, but kept pace for the garage. There was a duffle bag where Zach had stood, and he was running straight for me, full speed ahead.

Di and I kicked it up a notch. But a beautiful dark-haired girl with a full figure stepped next to Matt. The beauty said, "Where Zach running to? Who's zee blonde?"

"No one," Matt said.

I was no one to them? I ran faster. "Di, get to the car and open it."

We made it to the garage and I could hear footsteps getting closer. Di fumbled for her keys as I had the door handle in my hand, at the ready. "Di, now."

"Tatum? Tatum? Please, don't go. Wait. I can explain." Zach's plea carried through the garage.

My heart exploded all over again. I couldn't breathe. That asshole wouldn't stop killing me time and time again. "Get away." I couldn't be near him. Just hearing his voice gave me chest pains. And for a split second, his kisses ran through my mind. I just as quickly mentally erased them.

Di turned the key and flung her door open. She flipped the unlock switch. "Go."

I popped the handle and flung my door open and dropped down in the seat as Di started the car. I grabbed the door handle and pulled, but his hand stopped the door from closing.

He wasn't supposed to be back. I couldn't look at him. They'd sworn he wouldn't be. They swore he was living there and I should move on. I had. And now what? The jerk was back? I covered my face with my hands.

Di shifted the car. "Say it, Tate, and I'll drive off," she whispered.

"No. Please. I have to talk to you, Tatum. Give me two minutes. I've waited too long for you to run off."

I couldn't think fast enough, but a million things were going through my head at the same time, muffling my thoughts worse than watercolors dripping down a painting. Did I want to hear anything he had to say? "Time him, Di. Two minutes."

He squatted next to me, trying to see my face behind my hair. "I had no choice. Gramps made me go. As it is, I'm not really supposed to be back now, but with certain circumstances, the Leads voted to allow me to return, against Gramps's judgement. Things are screwed up for me, but I'm doing my best to work them out so we can be together again."

Not sure what made me explode, but I could feel the blood flowing to my cheeks. I slowly turned my head up at him, feeling my nostrils flaring. I tightened my lips to avoid biting them. My hands were wedged tightly under my legs, or I would have been too tempted to smack him upside his head. "You think for one minute I would give you, *us*, another chance? You must see 'moron' tattooed on my forehead."

His face aged. His eyes grew tired. "Tatum, I know you're mad."

"Mad? Mad? Did you get hit in the head with a baseball bat? Mad doesn't begin to describe what I feel. Or feel for you."

Zach reached for my hand, but I pulled away. "Don't you touch me. It's over. You up and left without saying anything. Nothing. You always promised me, Zach." The moment those words touched my lips, I felt them quiver. How could he leave me like he did? "Di, turn off the heat, I'm burning up."

"Tate, it's not on," she said.

"Look." He turned back toward the garage doors to the terminal, and then back to me. "They'll be coming soon. We're having dinner at Gramps's place, come with me, please? We can talk there."

I couldn't believe my ears. "Di, I think I've lost my

hearing or something, because this idiot believes I'd go with him to his family's restaurant."

Zach put his hand on my knee. I smacked it off. "I said, don't."

He placed his hand on my knee again and glared at me, getting close to my face. "You are *my* spoken for and if I want to touch you, I will. Now, I am asking you nicely to go to dinner with me. I want to talk to you. I have a plan, and there's a few things you need to hear from me. Not anyone else."

Zach had never spoken to me like that before. He spoke as if he controlled me, and that scared me shitless for the first time since I'd known him. I wasn't afraid he'd physically hurt me, but that he controlled me. *As if he owns me, and I'll die before I let that happen.*

I had to keep swallowing to breathe. His face would make me change my mind, so I looked out the front windshield. "You don't own me."

"Baby?" His hand came up to my face and cupped my cheek. I let him touch me, but I refused to look at him. "You have no clue how much I've wanted this face. This skin." He moved toward me.

I jerked away. "Don't. I mean it."

"Fine, but come with me?" He looked over at Di. "You wanna help me out here?"

She rested her arms over the steering wheel. "Look, you had your chance. Gramps blew it for you. And you know it. The sad thing is, Tate's already moving on with someone who doesn't make her deal with this Mob crap of yours."

"Di. Shhh," I said. "Don't say that word out loud. Someone could hear."

Di glanced around at the empty garage.

A low growl came from Zach's chest. "Who? That idiot, Nigel? You think *he's* going to make you happy over me?"

"Yeah, I do. As a matter of fact."

"Did you tell him about me?"

"That you're a prick? Yeah, I did."

"Still the loyal one. I knew you wouldn't say anything about my family," Zach said.

I turned to him. "Too bad only one of us understands the word—loyal."

"That's what I'm trying to tell you . . . we need to talk."

Voices echoing through the garage from the terminal doors caught our attention.

Zach shoved me forward and forced my seat up. An oomph escaped from my chest.

He climbed in back and dropped down on the floor. "Di, I'll give you a hundred bucks if you drive next to Matt or Bobby and tell them I left for The Hill already."

"Two hundred, and you have a deal." She looked at me, smiling. Bopping her eyebrows up and down.

"Fine, two. But don't pull too close so anyone can see me back here."

Zach folded his body and hunkered down in the backseat's floor well. I nodded, letting Di know that I agreed. Mom always said curiosity killed the cat. Time would tell if I was down to eight lives. Di backed her car out of the parking space and coasted through the garage.

Something was making Zach react this way, and maybe I did care what it was. After I found out, then I could go home.

Matt and Andi, with his parents, walked out first. Di pulled up to them, and I rolled down the window. "Um, hi. Zach already left for the Hill. He'll meet you all down there," I said.

Matt looked back at the glass sliding doors. "They're coming. Go."

Andi looked at me with eyes bigger than Pluto's.

Matt's dad looked back at the doors too, but whispered, "We'll cover. Hurry."

No one needed to tell Di twice. She drove off, away from the doors. We circled up to the top, exit level of the garage.

Di pulled up to an open lane. "This isn't free either, Zach. And get up, we're clear."

He threw himself on Di's backseat, reached in his back pocket, and took out his wallet. He pulled a twenty out for the parking and then counted an endless supply of twenties. "Here, for the parking. And then this is for getting me out of there."

Zach handed Di two hundred and twenty dollars. We paid the parking fee and Di drove through the gate and pulled over to the side. She counted a hundred and gave it to me.

I held the money in my hand. "Why are you giving me this? It's yours."

"No, now we have to do something with him. While we drive his sorry ass down to the Hill you're going to have to listen to all of his crap. That's gotta count for something."

"Oh." I didn't feel right taking payment to get him out of there. Besides, I didn't work for it, and then this wasn't just money, this was mob money. I handed it back. "I can't."

Di refused. "Yes, you can and you will."

"Tatum, take the damn money," Zach said.

Di shoved her share in her purse and drove off.

I put it in my wallet and sat there like the helpless little girl again. What was wrong with me? I thought I'd gotten past that feeling of *I've lost all control in my life.*

He leaned in between Di and me. "Now, look. I know you probably heard stuff about me, and I'm sure it's true—"

"Did you sleep with Mariacella?" came barreling out of my mouth. My face tightened, every inch of my body tightened. I dared him to say yes. Dared him.

Zach froze and took a long minute gazing into my eyes with a blank stare. "Yes."

I turned around and looked out the front. "This discussion is over." He made me feel cheap. A hiccup got stuck in my chest. If it dislodged, I would be crying. I took a few deep breaths and exhaled slowly, releasing the hiccup without the tears.

That was, until he put his hand on my shoulder. That was all it took to make what I'd felt about his leaving me and my finding out he'd slept with another girl come barreling from deep inside my heart. "You lied to me. You said you'd always be there for me. No matter what. Then you take off with no notice. No note. No phone message. Nothing. And then you screw someone else. I thought you loved me?" I spun in my seat, facing him. "Do you love her?"

Zach's eyes drooped. "No. To be honest, I hate her. If I could, I'd kill her."

"Don't say things like that." I wiped the snot from

my nose and decided to get a tissue. I found one in my purse. Maybe if he was grossed out by me, he'd leave me alone. It would make it easier on me. But no, not Zach.

"I'm sorry, Tate. I begged for forgiveness."

"Is that supposed to make me feel better? You begged who? Not me," I cried out.

He held my arm. "No, I'm sorry. I swear I didn't want it to happen, but had to . . . to get back here to you."

I didn't want to feel anything of his, especially his hands. "Who is this Mariacella?"

"The girl at the airport."

"*You brought her back with you?* And you're in the car with us? Oh my gosh . . . you've lost your got damn mind. Di, pull over," I yelled.

Di glanced at me for a hot second. "God damn?"

"You know I don't say 'God damn.'"

She shook her head. "Out of all the things to worry about. All right, I'll get off at the next exit. But what's your plan, Tate?"

"He's walking. I'm done."

Zach sighed. "No. Now, look. What I'm telling you is, I have a plan to get out of the wedding."

"*Wedding?*" I considered jumping out of the car in the middle of the highway. Why was I letting this happen to me?

"Yes, Gramps wants me to take over her father's enterprise. I can be Lead and do whatever I want. Her old man owns a vineyard—he owns a lot, actually. It's my way of getting us out. Out forever."

"Di, please tell me what I'm missing before I turn around and strangle him." The ugly cry made a second appearance. My nose wouldn't stop running. Not only was my nose already swollen, but I could feel my eyes were too.

"Zach, tell me you don't honestly think what you're saying is helping Tate understand what your plan is, because I do not understand either," Di said, glancing back in the rearview mirror.

"What I'm saying is, her father was just diagnosed with prostate cancer. Then when he dies, I will take over his enterprise and become a winemaker. With you, Tate."

"What about that girl, Zach? You're not making sense. She exists."

"Tate, I don't have to marry her. I can drag this out . . . maybe just until next summer. Then I become Lead, and no one tells me what to do. I ditch her but gain everything."

"Di, I have a headache. I want to go home."

"Tatum. I can make this work. I love you. If we don't do this together, I have nothing to live for."

I wiped my eyes, feeling a bit more in control of the crying machine. "I'm sorry you're going through this, God knows I am, but you can't possibly expect me to hang tight while you're engaged to another girl and screwing her. How dare you ask that of me?"

"I'm not, not anymore."

"You're not what? Engaged?"

"No. I just screwed her that one time."

I sat back in my seat, letting my body melt into the contours. Zach was breaking me down faster than he was talking. He spoke in such a vulgar way about being intimate with his fiancée. I would be devastated if the guy I was with spoke about me like that. This wasn't the Zach I knew. "I can't hang around and wait for an 'if.' Di is right. I've moved on." I looked at Zach. He wasn't the same guy, he was hard. This Zach scared me. "I'm in love with Nigel. And maybe he isn't you, but he sure doesn't have Mob crap for baggage."

Zach sat up, edging closer to me. "No. I don't believe it. You may feel infatuation for him, but you're not in love with him. I won't have it." He got that look in his eyes, the crazed Mob look. The look he had when he'd told me he could touch me if he wanted to.

Di pulled in front of the restaurant and parked. "Now what?"

I wouldn't look at him. I sat up straight and stared out the windshield. "Bye, Zach."

"Not without you. Come in and get dinner." Zach moved to Di's side of the car. She got out and moved her seat for him. Zach came around to my door and opened it. "I beg you with everything I have left in me, please come in?"

"Why?"

"How many times do I have to say we need to talk? And you can get dinner."

"I'm not hungry. Besides, you already talked, and it was longer than two minutes."

Zach squatted next to me, looking at me with dark, cold eyes. "I have been through hell this past month, and I would be forever grateful if I could spend just another hour with you before you go back to Nigel."

"So, you're accepting I'm with Nigel?" It appeared we were getting somewhere.

"I accept you're with him for now. But not for long."

"Zach, you're sweating." He had sweat beads around his neck. A droplet rolled down his neck. "You okay?"

"Tatum, if this is what it takes, I will pay you three hundred dollars if you will join me for dinner." He glanced up at me, his eyes heavy, empty, all sign of happiness gone.

Zach was breaking my heart. I wasn't madly in love with him anymore—at least I kept telling myself that—but I cared about him. This was *my* Zach, but it was clear he was struggling for anything he wanted in life. If this simple gesture of dinner and talking meant so much to him, then I'd do it. "Why would you offer to buy my company? I'm confused."

"I offered you money to show you how serious I am about your joining me."

"Don't ever offer to buy me again. It's insulting."

I got out of the car and Di grabbed her purse, saying, "I suppose we're going in?"

I couldn't help rolling my eyes, annoyed at myself for giving in. Di smiked, not saying a word to me.

This was the reason I liked her so much.

CHAPTER 3

Zach

A TRAIN OF CARS SAT IN front of the restaurant. *They're here.* "Let's go in. But I need you
to do me a favor, Tate. I need you to answer to your
middle name, Frances. Okay?"

I stared at her surprised face.

She stopped in the doorway, planting her feet.
"What now? Why?"

I bent closer to her face and whispered, "Because
my fiancée won't want to hear Tatum is here having
dinner with me."

"You asshole, let me out of here. I don't know what
I was thinking." Tatum pushed and shoved, trying to
get back out the door.

I grabbed her and held tight. "They're already here.
Get inside and play it cool. I'm sorry, but it has to
happen this way."

Tatum flung her back to the wall, inside the doorway, crying. "Why are you doing this to me? I don't
want to be in. I was out. You made sure I moved on.
This is torture for me. You have a fiancée . . ." She
covered her face with her hands.

Di hugged her, trying to whisper. "Tate, just go in. We can leave soon, I promise. Or I'll step in. I wanna meet this bitch fiancée of his."

Tatum was breaking my heart. I never wanted anyone else but her. This was no way to live. We were supposed to be getting out of the biz.

"Do you not hear yourself, Di? Zach's fiancée. Zach's *fiancée*."

Tatum stood there, still shedding tears. I looked out and saw the others were getting out of the cars and would be heading this way. I grabbed Tate and Di and pulled them inside. "For Christ's sake, please get in here. You can't be in the door when Gramps arrives."

"Gramps? Gramps?" Tatum swung her arms, striking me as fast and hard as she could. I could barely block. "I hate you. I hate you, Zacharia."

Di pulled Tatum toward the bathroom but gave me the look of death. "You are an asshole, Zach. I can't believe you're doing this." She turned back around. "Come on, Tate, let's clean you up a bit."

Outside the ladies' lounge, I could hear them. Di was giving Tatum a pep talk. "Tate, chin up. You can do this. That bitch has nothing . . ."

The truth was, Tatum didn't need a pep talk. Whether Di said those things or not, Tatum was smart enough to put her game face on. Di knew the family, and our fathers had never wanted to drag Officer Mancini's daughter into this lifestyle. My mom always said, though, that it was Di's destiny. I hadn't been sure I agreed with Mom until recently.

Moments later, Di flung the door open and stopped when she saw me standing there. She glared at me and mouthed, "Ass. Hole."

Tatum glanced up and the moment she saw me, she said, "Let's do this."

That's my girl.

Di walked behind Tate. I led them to the area of the dining room where we gathered for dinner. Most everyone was there. First thing was first. Tate had to meet my parents without Mariacella around. Matt noticed us first and I nodded my head, acknowledging his presence when he came over.

Matt came over. "What are you doing? You're suicidal."

"Get rid of Mariacella for a while. I need Tate to meet Mom and Dad."

"You're mental." Matt turned his attention to the girls. "Hi, Tatum. Di. Sorry you guys got dragged into this madness," he whispered.

"Any other name you want to call me before the shit hits the ceiling? Now, can you please go?"

Matt turned around and grabbed Andi's hand, whispering to her. She was another one giving me the death glare. She wouldn't be the last.

We waited off to the side while Matt and Andi got Mariacella to the ballroom upstairs, giving her a tour.

I grabbed Tatum's hand. It was sweaty. I glanced back at her and she was trying to hold it together. My baby was scared shitless. All I ever wanted to do was take this lifestyle and keep it away from her. "I love you."

She took a deep breath and ground her teeth, using her German blue eyes to rip me apart. So maybe it wasn't the best thing to say to her, but I did. She had no clue how deep my love for her was.

I escorted her up to my parents. They were doing

double takes between Di and Tatum.

Dad held up his arms and waved us over. "Here, over here."

We went to the farthest corner of the restaurant and Mom was already smiling wide. "Mom, please."

She nodded, anxious to put her hand out.

"Mom. Dad. This is *my* Tatum." I placed my hand on the middle of Tatum's back. Feeling her made me want to touch more of her. I had other things to worry about, but I couldn't ignore what effect my spoken for had on me.

Poor Tatum didn't even see it coming. My mom wrapped her arms around her and squeezed. "Heavens. You're exactly what I imagined." Mom backed away, but still held her arms. "My dear girl, we know this is anything but normal, or how we wanted to first meet you. But I promise you, Nicola and I are doing everything we can to break this deal."

Tatum backed up. "Don't let me be the reason you have trouble in your family." She looked at me. "I care about Zach. But this can't happen again."

Mom's excitement deflated as she carefully examined Tatum's face. I knew what she was doing— reading Tatum's facial expressions for her true feelings.

Dad stepped in. "Tatum, I'm Nicola. Zach's father."

"And this is Diane Mancini," I said.

Di put her hand out and hoisted her head high. "You can call me Di."

My dad looked at me, slightly bent forward. "Mancini?"

I feared they wouldn't want Officer Mancini's daughter joining us, but there was no other way to keep Tatum with me. If I survived this evening, maybe it could work. Maybe.

Mom looked at my dad and pulled her shoulders back, plastering her performance smile on her face. "Well, Di, what a pleasure to meet you too."

"Okay. Di it is, then. It's a pleasure," my dad said.

Di had to realize they knew who her father was from the looks on their faces. She couldn't glare at me hard enough.

Dad looked at me. "What's the plan, we can't say her name again?"

"This is Frances, Bobby's friend," I patted Tatum's shoulder.

Tatum flinched and took her elbow into my gut.

"Mr. and Mrs. Bertano, I am glad to finally meet you, but I will only pretend this one time. You must know, or at least can imagine, how I feel right now. We're not kidding anyone."

"Oh dear, we do. We can only imagine. And we are so sorry."

Dad waved his hand and Bobby came running over. He looked at me, then at Tate and Di, smiling. "Hi, Tate. Didn't expect to see you tonight."

"Bob, we don't have but a second. This is Frances, and she's your friend from school. You asked her to join us for dinner since you've been gone so long and missed her."

Bobby snickered. "All right. I'm with Tate. Di?"

"Yeah, she's Frances's friend. You asked her too."

"My lucky day." Bobby took Tate's hand and pulled her away from me. Di took Bobby's other arm, playing along. Tate glanced back, but not long enough for me to say *I love you* again.

Dad jerked his entire body in front of me. "What

are you thinking? Bringing that poor girl here in this mess? With Mariacella? If Gramps finds out *that's* Tatum . . . our heads will roll. And you bring Officer Mancini's daughter into this? I told you to get off that shit. You're not thinking clearly. Then if Maria—"

"Dad, I'm off it. I haven't used since our talk. Trust me. But when I saw Tate at the airport, I couldn't just let her leave. It's been six weeks. Six weeks with no contact."

My mother squeezed my father's arm in warning. "Nic, it's not going to help to yell at him now. We need to keep Tate and Mariacella away from each other." Mom glared at me like I should have known better, and I should have. "Mariacella would stab her in the back. Poor girl wouldn't know where to begin protecting herself. This is a mess, Zacharia. A bona fide mess."

"Mom, I have to be near her. You know this is—"

Dad leaned in and whispered, "Just keep the two apart. Mariacella isn't stupid. She'll see how you're reacting to Tatum. And then God help the little German girl. You better make this convincing."

So in other words, no pressure. Because I could never hide my feelings for Tatum well.

If at all.

CHAPTER 4

Tatum

BOBBY TOOK MY WAIST AND led me away from Zach and his parents. I just glanced back. That asshole was making my life a living hell. I wanted to eat so Di could take me home, away from Zach.

Bobby leaned over to me. "Tatum, don't worry. If Nicola and Catwoman are in on it, it'll be fine."

I looked at Bobby, waiting for him to look at me. "Take me to the bar. I need a drink."

"Whohohoa. All right. Little Tatey . . . I mean, Frances is loosening up. Di, you game?"

"Yup." Di held onto Bobby's other arm.

We stepped up to the bar and Bob ran behind it, then leaned over the countertop toward us. "What'll it be, ladies?"

"Hot Damn shots. I need something strong to do this," I said, glancing back at Zach. It appeared his parents were not happy about something. Good.

"Seriously?" Bobby's tone was calm.

I turned back to him. He wasn't moving, just waiting for me to answer him. "Yeah. Seriously. Does anybody care what this is like for me?"

Bobby grabbed the bottle, set up three shot glasses, and poured. "Frances, I have a good idea. But it doesn't make it easier." Bobby put the bottle back and handed us each a glass. Then he took his own. "To better times," he said, tossing the shot back.

Di and I followed his lead, then just as quickly we were blowing fire out of our mouths just like the night before.

I put my shot glass down and leaned closer to the bar edge. "And would you like to tell me why you were a complete dickhead the last time I saw you? Before holiday break?"

Bobby glanced at me, then moved his eyes to our surroundings. "Gramps. He made me. Sorry. Change the subject."

Without fail it always went back to the one-word subject—Gramps.

Andi joined us. "So, it's come to this? Shots?"

"Yup. If that asshole is going to do this to me, then so be it."

Andi leaned closer to me. "She's over there. And she's intrigued by who the blonde is. She asked me if I knew who you are and I said I wasn't exactly sure, but someone from school, I'd forgotten your name. Look . . . she must feel threatened by you. But she has no idea who you are. So can you tell me what's going on?"

"Good, let her feel threatened, because this is me and Bobby's friend, Frances," Di said.

Andi's eyes expanded, then blinked a hundred times. "You've got to be kidding me."

Bobby poured another round. "Not kidding, she's my fun for the night." He winked. "So is Lady Di here."

Andi shook her head. "You better pour me one. I had to pretend to not want to kill her upstairs in the ballroom. Which, by the way, is beautiful."

"Thanks. Grandma Cecilia decorated it. Anything elegant, classy, Grandma does."

"Gramps's wife? Your grandma?" I asked.

"Yeah. She stays away a lot. She hates how things are." He shrugged, pouring Andi a glass. "She's very small and petite." Bobby glanced up at me. "Like you, Frances." He put the bottle back up and turned around to us. He raised his glass. We followed.

"Salute." We tossed them back, and the liquor scorched another hot trail down my throat.

Matt walked up to us, and his hand found Andi's waist. "Shots? Don't get trashed before dinner. You all need to be Oscar winners tonight."

"We know," Bobby said. "Matt, you remember my good friends from school? Frances and Di? I asked them to join me for dinner."

Matt took a deep breath and mumbled, "It better work. She's feeling left out. Tyler is talking to her now, but he and Sergio can only keep her occupied for so long."

"Pshaw. If my dad is on the job, she'll want to marry him instead of Zach by the time he's done with her."

"Dinner is served."

We looked to where the voice came from. A guy wearing a chef's hat and a white cooking jacket stood by the door to the kitchen.

Bobby came around the bar and took my hand and Di's. "Let's go, Frances. Showtime."

My heart began doing the *Flashdance* warm-up on

its own.

Bobby walked Di and me around the table to the back, wall side. He sat between Di and me. Catalina, Zach's mom, sat next to me with Nicola on her other side. But across from me, between Matt and Zach, was Mariacella.

I leaned over to Bobby's ear. "Did the seating have to be done like this?"

"We already have our seats. Our guests sit around us."

I could feel a glare on me, like someone was using their Superman heat vision, burning a hole through me. I knew who it was, and I would have to buck up and face the music. My ex was engaged to her. That lump came back to my throat. I couldn't cry here, not like this. Screw it. If this girl was better suited for Zach than me, I wanted to know and see what she had had that I didn't. Besides Italian blood.

I took a deep breath and raised my head with a smile on my face.

Sure enough, Mariacella was staring at me so I put on my big girl panties and performed. I shot my hand out to her, over the table. "Hi, I'm Frances, Bobby's friend from school."

Mariacella's glare faded and a bright smile appeared. She shook my hand. "Si. Yes, Bobby's girl. Nize to meet you . . . uh . . .uh, Flances. You the girl from the airport."

She couldn't even pronounce my name right with her strong accent. It was hard to understand her.

"Sorry. I got the meeting place wrong." *Why couldn't I come up with something more clever?*

"I'm Zacharia's *fidanzato*, Mariacella." She flung

her hand out to Zach's chest. He sat there with his hat so far down I couldn't see his eyes.

A bit of vomit hurled up my esophagus and then got stuck. With a strong swallow, I forced it back down. I assumed fidanzato meant fiancée.

Di shot her hand over the table next. "I'm Di, Bobby's friend too. How wonderful to meet Zach's fiancée. I mean . . . wow . . . so young . . . and to be engaged."

In that moment it was clear Di was taking the Oscar home. I envied her ability to play cool. Of course, it wasn't her ex sitting in front of her with his full-figured fiancée. *Why couldn't I have inherited my grandma's physique?*

The rest of the family was gathering around the table, not missing a beat. Nowhere did I see Gramps, though. Meeting him would be the nail in my coffin. *Just breathe.*

I wanted to look at Zach again, but I didn't. I could feel he was dying inside. He had his shoulders slumped and his head down—his typical invisible posture. A ball cap hung low over his eyes.

Suddenly, under the table, Catalina tapped my knee. Nothing else. Weird behavior. She just gave me a little tap and didn't even look my way. I didn't consider glancing at her.

"Oh Baldassario, you have many girls. I know you type," Mariacella mocked.

"Baldassario?" I whispered to him.

Bobby behaved as if his dirty little secret was spilled. "Mariacella, we told you we don't use our blood names here in the US. Just call me Bobby. Please."

"Yes, I agree, Mariacella. If you're staying the month

with us, please call the boys by the names they prefer. It just keeps harmony in my house," Catalina said.

A month? My hairline felt moist. Again.

The man who'd been on the TV news the day before I'd broken up with Zach took a seat on Di's other side—Bobby's dad, who had been taken in for questioning for money laundering.

It wasn't what I should have been thinking, but he was very attractive. They all were. Even Zach's dad, Nicola, if I was being honest with myself.

Zach stood up and walked over to the bar. Of course we watched him. He grabbed the bottle of Hot Damn and came back and placed it in front of me. "I saw Bob pouring for you earlier. Don't be shy."

Mariacella wrapped her arms around Zach and smiled. "You so thoughtful."

Zach again ignored her.

Bobby grabbed the bottle and poured an amount equal to a shot into my wineglass. "Here, Frances. You'll want another when we toast to the happy couple."

"Huh?"

I looked around Bobby for Di. She held her head with narrowed eyes. I glanced to Matt's other side and Andi was doing the same thing. Not knowing how to respond, we were SOL. Everyone would be toasting my ex and his new fiancée. A fiancée who still hadn't impressed me. She wasn't going to cure AIDS or win a Nobel Peace Prize. Not that I would, I just didn't see what this girl had over me. So she could speak Italian, I could learn. I could even get a spray tan and color my hair black. Okay, she had hips and boobs—big boobs. But I could get those too.

"Ciao, family." A man's deep voice came from the head of the table.

I looked down the twenty-top table and saw an elderly version of Nicola. Jesus. That had to be Gramps.

Again, Catalina patted my knee and then nothing.

"I happy we brought back Zach's fiancée with us for the month. My youngest grandson is marrying the perfect Italian woman. Mariacella, say hi to our family. You'll be one of us soon."

She popped out of her seat and waved. Her boobs bounced when she jumped. Those were just too darn big. I mean, really. And Zach had had his hands all over those boobs. I wanted to pull mine up in my Wonderbra, because there was no wonder. *You can't even tell I have boobs in this stupid sweater. I gotta burn it when I get home.*

Catalina patted my knee again. This time I looked at her. She didn't acknowledge me above the table. *What gives?*

She took a deep breath, but exposed a forced grin aimed right at Mariacella. Then it hit me. She was trying to give me support, but showing face to Mariacella and the family.

Catalina patted my knee again.

Dear Lord, was I right?

How did she know what I could be thinking? Then again, it wouldn't take a genius to see this was one big act.

"Ciao, Bertanos. I Mariacella, Zacharia's fidanzato. I'm so happy to be a part of your beautiful family." She waved to Gramps and sat back down. She pulled her own chair in and looked at Zach. He ignored her.

She gave him a dirty look, then mumbled, "*Stai bevendo troppo di nuovo.*"

That was a mouthful of *what the heck did that mean?*

Catalina leaned over to my ear. I backed up, but stopped and moved forward to meet her. "He's drinking too much again," Catalina whispered.

He is. I noticed how often he's poured. I had a couple of shots, but he's had doubles. I examined Zach.

Hat over his face—he wasn't his normal confident self—he wanted to melt away into the walls.

Catalina's hand went to my knee and stayed. She turned her head to me and mouthed, "Maybe you can help him stop."

Drinking? Zach's occasional beer was one thing, drinking shot after shot of hard liquor was another. This was a nightmare. If only I could blink and open my eyes to find myself in my bedroom. This was a lot to process. Were they telling me Zach had been drinking a lot, and often? Mariacella didn't tell him to slow down or stop, just complained when his drunken behavior offended her. Otherwise, she didn't seem to care much about anything. He could drink himself into oblivion as far as she was concerned. Did she even love Zach? Why was she marrying him, and marrying into this family? None of this made sense. Then out of all people, his mom wanted me to "help" him? Why couldn't his fiancée help him stop drinking? Who was going to help me?

"Thank you, my dear Mariacella. Now, I see Bobby has two friends here tonight."

Bobby held his hand out. "This is Frances and—"

"Baldassario, stop. These not how we do things here," Gramps interrupted.

Bobby looked at me. "You have to stand. I'm sorry," he whispered.

From behind I was pinched in the ass. I yipped and popped up out of my chair, holding my rear. I looked back and Catalina had the same shit-stirring grin Zach used to have.

"Um, hi. I'm Frances, Bobby's friend from school. It's nice to meet his family. Thanks for having me for dinner. Happy New Year."

Everyone at the table reciprocated the sentiment.

I leaned back to sit.

"Wait." Gramps called out. "You our Baldassario's friend? You seem familiar."

I stood back up and began to sweat, rubbing my fingers across my forehead. "I'm his friend, yes. But not sure why I would be familiar to you. Sorry."

Gramps grinned and let me be.

Di stood up next and introduced herself, leaving out her last name.

Gramps laughed. "My dear, *you* are familiar. What did you say your last name is?"

Nicola flashed a dirty look at Zach, before turning his attention to Di.

"Uh, Mancini. I'm Diane Mancini."

"Now, you we know. Nicola, aren't you friends with her pops? Officer Mancini?"

"Yes, Gramps. We go back a ways."

Gramps clapped his hands together. "*Perfetto*, Baldassario. We approve."

Everyone around me seemed surprised Gramps thought it was a good thing. Di didn't skip a beat and sat down.

"*Buona*. Good. Now we toast and eat." Everyone

raised their wineglasses. Di, Andi, and I raised our wineglasses with a shot of Hot Damn in each. "Welcome, new friends. And congratulations to Zacharia and Mariacella on their engagement. I look forward to this summer's wedding. Salute."

Everyone toasted with Gramps.

Di, Andi, and I pretended to, but didn't. We appeared to be on the same wavelength.

"Third time is a charm," I whispered.

Di and Andi repeated together. "Third time is a charm. Salute." We tossed them back.

A herd of waiters and waitresses came rushing out with plates in their hands. They put a pork sausage dish in front of me. One whiff and I wanted to vomit. I couldn't eat that.

"Dear, what is it?" Catalina asked me.

Zach looked up for the first time and his stare went straight to his mother's. "Mom, she doesn't eat meat. I thought I mentioned—"

"No, I told Cat," Bob interrupted Zach. "Stan?" A waiter came back over and bent down to him. "Stan, Frances here doesn't eat beef or pork. Can you throw a vegetarian or maybe a seafood dish together for her?"

Everyone around me seemed to scramble, except Mariacella. She sat there glaring at Zach.

"Of course, sir. Right out, miss." The waiter bowed and then took off.

Cat jumped up. "I'm sorry, Bob. You did tell me your friend is a partial vegetarian. I'll be right back with a salad, Frances."

"No. I'm fine with bread. Really."

Catalina ignored me and continued towards the

swinging doors.

"How you know how she eats?" Mariacella asked Zach.

"Not many people at school are partial vegetarians. Leave me alone," Zach hovered over his plate.

Mariacella turned her attention back to me and a wicked grin spread across her face. "You vegetarian?"

The expression in her eyes ran a cold chill down my spine. This would bite me in the ass. So I wanted to kill her with kindness, determined to earn my Oscar. "I am. Just don't care for meat."

"How could you not care for meat?" She looked at Zach and laughed. "A woman should want a big sausage. Right, love?" Her hand went below the table.

Zach's fiancée was laughing at me because I didn't eat meat?

He jumped with wide eyes. His hand went below the table. "Cut it out. Just because you'll put anything in your mouth doesn't mean other women will."

Zach would be in the doghouse after that. But no one said anything about the exchange between him and his fiancée. I found it weird. He wasn't loving or caring toward her. He was cold and distant, down-right mean. Could the honeymoon have already ended?

"You ass," Mariacella said and then began eating.

After dinner, it was time to make my escape. I started playing the "I'm tired" bit. "Well, Bobby, it was nice. Thanks for inviting me and Di."

Bobby stepped up to me and wrapped his arms around me. He whispered in my ear, "You did great. I know they're proud of you."

"Thanks. But I only did it to keep the peace. Zach

isn't the man I fell in love with. It's over between us."
I kissed the side of Bobby's head and pulled away.

Di jumped in to say goodbye next. I began to think
she was milking this "friend from school" cow.

Zach kept staring at me from a bar chair. He had
been drinking heavily during dinner. It took everything I had to turn away from him, not wanting to
make things worse for any of us. Andi and Matt came
over and said goodbye, but Andi asked if we could
run her home on our way. She didn't want to wait
on Matt. But Di and I both knew she wanted to talk
about the *fiancée*.

Zach whispered in Tyler's ear. Tyler backed away
and glanced over at me with a gentle nod. Tyler
walked over to Mariacella and slid his arm around
her waist, she seemed to enjoy his attention. He led
her out of the room.

The moment they were out of sight, Zach ran over
to me. "Come with me, quick, before she gets bored."
Zach didn't wait for an answer. He took my hand and
pulled me in the opposite direction and down their
service hall. He opened a door and flipped the light
switch. I spun around. We were in a storage room of
dry goods.

"Tatum, please bear with me. You see the hell I'm
going through."

Good, we were alone. "What you're going through?
Are you blind? So this was just a typical night out for
me? You're an ass."

He grabbed his shirt sleeves, one at a time, and
folded them up, exposing his forearms. There in fresh
black ink was a big black heart with wings. One
arm said, *Zach*. The other had my name, *Tatum*. Then

underneath it said, *made for each other*, two words on each arm.

"You see this?" He held his arms together, making one heart.

I backed away, one slow step at a time. "No. No, why would you do that? That's crazy. That's forever, Zach."

"Because that's how I feel. In Italy it was my way of reminding them of my commitment. It didn't matter how many times they made me go out with her. I'm in love with you, baby. Always will be."

"A tattoo? What is she going to say?"

"She knows. She saw it the night I got it."

"And she's okay with it?"

"She has no choice. They can't do anything about the tat now, but she nags me about *my Tatum* any chance she gets. Trust me, I've had to listen to her bitch about it for a couple of weeks. Look," Zach backed me up to the wall, his hands on my hips. "I get you want to kill me, and trust me, I'm not too happy with myself right now either. But together, we can make this work. It'll take time."

My back thudded. I couldn't get away. He had me pinned there. Zach held his body against mine. "I've missed you, baby. So much. Packing my bags . . . knowing I couldn't call you to let you know Gramps was shipping me out . . . I hated myself. And every damn minute I was over there, they had hawk eyes on me. I couldn't pick up the phone to call my parents without Vito listening in. Gramps forbid any contact. I was going mad. Then when I saw you at the airport . . . there was no way in hell I was letting you run from me."

Zach raised both of his hands and cupped my cheeks. Seeing those perfect lips form into happiness for the first time since he'd gotten off the plane made me weak at the knees. Thankfully I had the wall for support.

"I love you. You're the only thing that makes me happy. The only thing."

He lowered his mouth to mine and kissed me. The old zing he'd once created came out of its dormant state and spiraled through my body like a dancing orb. He felt good. His lips were immediately familiar, exactly the way I remembered them. An intimidating heat radiated between us.

Zach took his hands over my shoulders and then down my arms. He pushed his body against mine as far as he could go, and then took his hands under my ass and lifted me.

"Fuck," he moaned.

No. What was I doing? I had to stop him. I backed away the inch he allowed between our heads, mumbling between our lips, "Zach, stop. Now."

If his return had happened three weeks earlier, I would have taken him back, but not now. I missed Nigel. I wanted Nigel to kiss me like that.

Being loyal was my signature. That applied to everything. Not just the Bertanos' secret lifestyle. I had a boyfriend, and it wasn't Zach.

Zach backed away, breathing fast. He let me slide back down and turned away from me. "I miss you. Why can't you see how much I hate this," Zach grunted.

The door popped open and Bobby came inside and just as quickly shut the door behind him. "She's asking for you, Zach. Frances, it's time."

I stood in front of Zach. "Goodnight. I'm sorry. I really am. Will I see you in school tomorrow?"

He looked up at me, his eyes redder than those of a meth head who hasn't slept for three days. "Yes. I'll see you in the morning. I can't wait." Zach put his arms around me. "Goodnight, Tatum. I love you. I love you so much."

There was nothing else to say.

Bobby followed me out of the storage room. "He'll be okay. Let's see how he is at school in the morning. You and Di drive safe." He gave me a quick hug.

I turned around to look for Di but found Mariacella in my face. She was like the plague. "Um, hi, Mariacella. Nice meeting you tonight." I wanted to scour my lips free of the poison that just spewed out of them.

"You too, Flances. I hope we be friends. When Baldassario comes to home, maybe you come with him?"

"Yeah. Maybe." Some foreign rage shot through my core. Over my dead body would I ever be friends with that bitch. She'd taken my boyfriend and screwed him. Then she made him her fiancée. I didn't care to ever see her again.

Di walked up and pulled my arm. "Night, everyone."

Andi joined us and the three of us walked out of the restaurant. The moment we dropped in Di's car we all bent over, gasping for air.

CHAPTER 5

Tatum

DI DROVE AWAY FROM THE Hill in record-breaking time, and within a few minutes we were on the highway heading back to North St. Louis County.

"So what did Zach say to you in that room? You guys weren't in there long, but when Mariacella didn't see him on the bar seat . . . ohh, she got upset," Di said.

Andi moved between our seats up front. "Yeah, like I said, she did the same thing when we came down from the ballroom. She's very suspicious. Like she's waiting for Zach to run off with another girl or something."

"Well, maybe because the idiot put a tattoo on his arms with our names, saying we were made for each other."

"No way." Di glanced at me.

"Yeah, Matt told me about it." Andi's voice lacked emotion.

"Well, that's one of the things we talked about in the room. He showed me his tattoos with my name written across his arm. Obviously, I was upset and asked why he did it. He said it's to remind them that he loves me. He's wearing his feelings on his sleeve, in a way. And the kicker is, she knows about the tats."

"Get out!" Di had a hard time staying focused on the road.

"Really, she knows and evidently doesn't care."

"I think she *does* care, and that's why she was overly protective of him tonight," Andi said.

"Yeah, you're probably right about that." The obvious didn't make me feel any better.

Di shook her head and didn't say another word.

A few minutes after we dropped Andi off, Di turned onto my street and glanced over at me. "Tate, I can only imagine what you're feeling, but believe me when I say not falling for Zach again is best right now. Give Nigel a chance. I know you still have feelings for Zach, but don't rush into something. His life is too screwed up and, to be honest, it's dangerous. You don't want to screw with Mariacella."

"No worries. I have no desire to get back on that wagon."

"You were always a terrible liar. Why do you and Zach think you guys can hide your true feelings for each other? Everyone can see it."

"Whether I do or not, I won't act on them. The Zach I fell in love with is gone."

"Good, you need to keep thinking that way, Tate. Because the thing is, the Bertanos never leave. Just look at Bobby. Where's his mom?"

"I don't know. Now that you mention it . . . where is she?"

Di slowed into my subdivision. "Exactly. Where is

she? No one knows, but what we do know is that she cheated on Sergio. She's been missing for years. I can't stress enough . . . be careful. Look . . . Nigel's here."

I took my gawking stare off her and looked out the windshield. Nigel's car was parked in front of my house. Without thinking, I took a deep breath. It was only seven thirty and I was exhausted.

Di pulled over. "This is between the two of us, but you know that."

I leaned over to give her a hug. "Thanks for being here, Di. Don't know what I'd do without you."

"I've said it before, honey bunches . . . you're always gonna need me." She hugged me back and waved to Nigel.

He opened my door and took my hand and I gave him a strong hug.

"Hey . . . you okay?" he asked.

With my face inches from his, I whispered, "Just happy to be home."

Happy to be back among the normal. The safe and comfortable lifestyle Nigel gave me. No matter what Zach and I had, I could never live like that—always on the edge of my seat.

CHAPTER 6

Tatum

THE FIRST DAY OF SCHOOL after the New Year was always the hardest, and walking into school and seeing Zach at my locker was unbearable. It was something he did for months before he left me. And there he stood, standing the way he always did—his back and right foot resting against the wall, head tilted upward, not talking to a soul. It broke my heart. We could never go back to that time when seeing him like that spun my heartbeat into a tilt-a-whirl.

Andi wasn't around. Nice to be semi-alone to get whatever this was out of the way.

I stepped up to my locker, and Zach came closer. "Tate, hi."

"Morning, Zach." I couldn't look at him, not yet. I had to plant my feet.

He leaned down to me. "I know you're probably not happy to see me, but nothing can ruin the mood I'm in. I'm relieved to be back."

I closed my locker and faced him. For some odd reason, I wasn't hesitant to confront him anymore.

He was going to make this awkward between us, and that didn't sit right with me.

"Good. I'm glad you're happy. See ya." I turned.

He grabbed my arm. "Don't. Don't shut me out."

In that instant, my internal furnace clicked on and I felt moisture on the back of my neck. "Neither you nor your family will ever control me. Got it? Now, take your hand off me."

His stare met mine and I saw his glassy red eyes. He drank before school. I took a deep breath to slow my anger from spewing out. "I know your secret. And I will not deal with your crap. You are not the guy I fell in love with," I said through gritted teeth. I flung my arm free of his grip.

"How do you know?"

I kept my voice down. "Do you not look in the mirror after you throw back a drink? I know."

"Tatum, look . . . it's just to help—"

"That stuff never helps. You know better. It's pathetic. It's weak. It's not *my* Zach."

He grabbed my body and pulled me into his chest. "Baby. I'm sorry."

I shoved back. "Don't be. Apologies are even weaker. There's no excuse."

Zach held my shoulders. "I beg you, work with me. We can take over the vineyards. Be patient."

Patience was not one of my stronger suits. I wanted to help him if I could, but if he saw a weakness in me, he'd use it to get his way. "All right. You come by my house after school since we didn't get the opportunity to talk last night. Don't put the bottle up to your lips any more today. And so we're clear . . . you better not bring your fidanzato."

"Oh my God . . . how do you know Italian?"

"I'm not an idiot. *She* was using the word last night. And wipe that stupid smile off your face. I'm going to class now."

During lunch I planned on going to the library to pick up an Italian reference book.

He annoyingly paraded behind me. "We might as well walk together. I'm in every class of yours, even third hour Child Development."

I cringed but kept walking.

Somehow the school day flew by, and now I paced my bedroom floor waiting for Zach, nervous but determined. I was ready. No clue what bullshit I would have to let enter my ears, but I was ready for an abundance.

My mom phoned when I walked in the door, letting me know she and my dad weren't coming straight home. Dad had forgotten to get his car tags, so they were going to the DMV. The phone rang again a few minutes later.

I sat on the edge of my bed. "Hello?"

"Love?"

"Nigel! Hi." Hearing his voice brought a peace within me. I let my body roll back into the waterbed.

"How was school?" he asked.

"Uh, okay. You?"

"First day back is always horrific. You want me to come over?"

"Sure. But later?" Much later, since Zach was coming over.

"Five-ish?"

"Perfect. See ya then, Nige."

No sooner had I hung up with Nigel than I heard the rumble.

I had a conference with my dresser mirror. Hands gripping the edge of the dresser, with elbows locked, I stared at myself. "Do not let him get to you. He's changed. He screwed another girl. It's not the Zach you once loved. He's drinking, he'll manipulate you. Don't trust him." *Yup . . . keep telling yourself that, Tatum. Get mad at him for ruining your relationship, because if you don't, you'll let him give you one sweet glance and you'll do whatever he wants. He's an asshole. Be strong. Plant those feet. For the love of God, plant those feet.*

I let him in the house and we went to my bedroom. He leaned on my dresser, facing me. That's when I examined him. Ball cap on—eyes shadowed—he wouldn't look me in the eye.

I got up to his face and stared. "What was our deal?"

He put his hands on my hips. "I've missed you so much. Do you have any clue how much I've wanted to see this face?" He cupped my cheeks. "Don't turn away from me. Please."

His warm hands sent that dormant monster of desire to my chest. "Don't you do this to me, Zach. We need to talk about your drinking. What's going on? And be honest about it. When and how often?"

"Whenever I have to see her. So this morning and after school when I ran home to get my car. But all day when I was in Italy. It was hell."

It made sense why he turned to the bottle. "So you keep it on you?"

"Always have something on me."

"Hand it over. I wanna see what you drink. This is

it. Own up to it, Zach. Step one."

He walked out. Just like that. He turned and walked out on me. I stood there dumbfounded. He didn't want to give it . . . it was easier to walk out.

I heard the front door again, and he stepped back in my room. He carried a liter of Scotch and handed me the bottle. We weren't talking about a beer or two—this was nasty, strong alcohol. I was familiar with alcoholism, since it ran in my family. Not to mention most of my friends had an uncle or some-body in their family who was an alcoholic too.

I looked up at him. "Why would you do this? You're better than this." That was a lot of pain to hold.

"Tate, don't cry. I know—"

"If you know, then why are you doing this?"

He stepped closer. "Were you shipped out of the country for reasons you don't agree with? Are you engaged to someone you want to kill?"

"I get it. Things suck for you right now. But yes, I have been forced, and I didn't drink to mask my pain. I used life to heal me. But yeah, I get when you're down, you're down. It feels terrible."

I stood before him and placed my free hand on his cheek. "But I began seeing you. You were my way of healing. You helped me and you didn't even know it. So many times I wanted to tell you how damaged I was. You eventually found out anyway."

He turned his head and kissed the palm of my hand.

"Is this the only bottle you have on you?"

"Yeah. I don't keep stuff in my room. It's on me."

My heart broke in two. "Zach, listen to me, I'm serious. With this"—I lifted the half-empty bot-tle—"you will never take over the vineyards. You will never be free of Mariacella." I couldn't face him. "You. Will. Never. Have. Me."

I met his stare. His face went blank. Hearing the words come out scared me worse than what I held in my hand.

I shoved past him and ran into the bathroom, locking the bolt behind me. I wasn't going to let him throw his life away. Not if I could help it.

Zach's footsteps came barreling to the bathroom door, followed by banging. "Tatum? What are you doing? Open up."

I couldn't breathe. I held Zach's awful future in my hand. But that wasn't what scared me. Zach's temper did.

"Step two." I said loudly. "Don't have any alcohol in your possession."

"Tatum, not funny. Open up, sweetheart."

I flipped up the toilet lid. "How much was this, Zach?"

"Tatum?" He jiggled the doorknob and shoved. "Sweetheart? A lot, it's the Black Label. Open the door."

"Zach, how much am I worth?"

It sounded like a head thudded on what stood between us. "Priceless." His breathing was heavy.

"Zach, choose now. Me or the drink?" *What am I doing? Am I actually going to pour this?* "I mean it, Zach. Choose now. Which is it?"

"You, but don't flush, please?"

"You can't have both." I took off the cap and with one flick of my wrist, the bottle began emptying. If I thought any more about what was happening, I wouldn't have poured.

The door shook from Zach trying to get inside. The room smelled worse than a dirty bar. How could he drink that? I hurried and pressed the lever. I stood there watching the last drop disappear and then refilling with fresh blue-tinted water. The Lysol drop-in smelled better too.

"Tatum, open this door."

I unlocked the door and he rushed inside and stood before a clean toilet. "The whole bottle?" He turned around and glared at the empty bottle in my hand before looking at my face. "It's gone?"

I was up against the wall. "Yes. You chose me. You made your choice. So from here on out you won't touch the crap or I will never speak to you again. Don't go buying any either, I'll know."

He stormed out of the bathroom and stomped his way into my bedroom where he paced the floor.

I gave him the empty bottle. "I can't throw the bottle out here. Take it home."

"Do you know what it's going to be like dealing with her without a drink?"

I stood still. His temper warned me to let him work this out. "Zach, please don't tell me you love that crap more than me."

"What? No."

"Then why do you act like it?"

Zach paused for a few minutes before taking small steps toward me with precise conviction. "You're right." He placed his hands on my hips.

"If you love me more, and you're not addicted, just broken, then why do you act otherwise? Why does that have so much control?"

"Control?" he whispered and glanced up to the

ceiling. "You're totally right. I won't let it control me anymore. Gramps does that enough."

"Right. So be stronger than the drink. *Be stronger than Gramps. Be you.*"

Zach grabbed my face and kissed me. "You are so right. I love you." He gently walked me back to my bed and sat me down. "Tatum, I want you to know something else."

"What?" His hands wrapped around my waist sent the dormant monster back into the whirling Tasmanian devil in my chest. The monster wanted out.

I could feel my breathing hitch. Zach was my undoing.

No. I had to plant my feet. Okay. Planted.

Zach pushed my back to the mattress. "After Kyle showed up here that night, I put security at your windows. I'd do anything for you."

He did what? Security at my windows? I should have been pissed, but I wasn't. "Why would you do that?"

"No one, especially not Kyle, will ever lay a hand on you." His voice was smoother than the Dove chocolates my mom would buy.

Zach crawled next to me and placed his body parallel to mine. I didn't need him that close to me. It was hard enough as it was to fight off how I much I wanted him.

"That's rather sweet. Thank you." *What did I say before he got here?* No clue because I saw my Zach emerging. My Zach was coming back to me. I missed him. The aura between us was lighting. He was calming, which relaxed me.

We lay there staring into each other's eyes. Every last good memory I had of him ran through my mind—our first dance, which led to my very first kiss—Homecoming, where we made out in his car—when he stood up for my honor when Kyle wanted to destroy my reputation—when I straddled his lap for the first time—when he had me against the wall, taking my shirt off—every waking moment with him. I needed *that* Zach.

He inched his face to mine. "I love you, Tatum Frances Duncan."

I didn't think before we kissed. He held the sides of my head and took my lips with his. Zach slid his body over mine.

With his body wrapped around mine, the Tasmanian devil of comfort whirled from my chest and cased my body, making my hands go to Zach's waist and pull. I wasn't thinking with my head, only the heart. The zing he created sprang from my toes to my head and knocked any and all sense out of my mind.

A slight parting of his bottom lip and he slid his tongue into my mouth. My feet went numb. Then my legs. But not my hips.

A low moan came from Zach and he slid his hands down my arms before pushing them up my shirt and grabbing my breasts. His scent of expensive sandalwood cologne stimulated my senses, driving me insane. Zach was making me forget about everything.

Nothing felt better on my skin than his warm hands and the tension in his fingertips.

The thought of the next step with him made me find my feet. I wanted more of him, from him, and he was ready to give me whatever I wanted. But if I did . . . I'd be in the Mob and not only deal with Mariacella, but Gramps too. Then there was Nigel. If

I chose Zach, the decision would mean sacrificing my life. I would be giving up everything—most of all, control.

Zach sat up. Seeing the way he was looking at me made me realize my conscience wasn't the only thing to grow.

I couldn't.

There was Nigel.

Nigel was the smart, safe choice. Zach was a dangerous Mob choice.

"Tatum, I love you." He came down to my neck, his lips trailing kisses on my bare skin.

My breathing hitched and my hips betrayed me again, moving to the motion of his.

No. This was going too far. Would I break up with Nigel for a life in the Mob, forever? I didn't know. No. Maybe.

"Oh, Zach." A moan came out.

Darn, now my head was betraying me again. *Okay, do it now. Ignore the way he's making my skin melt into his mouth. Making my skin melt between his lips . . .*

"Zach." It came out hushed.

"Baby?" he mumbled against my skin.

"Don't call me baby. I don't like it." He'd never called me baby before he'd left for Italy.

Zach froze. "No?"

"Can you sit up?" Yes, my head was finally working and taking back control.

We looked at each other. "Zach, I can't. I'm sorry."

"Look, I'm getting rid of her, it's just a matter of time."

I wiggled out from underneath him and grabbed my sweater, pulling it over my head. "Okay, where do I even begin to say what's wrong with that statement?"

I climbed out of the waterbed, but Zach stayed put and flopped to his back. I had to keep my stare away from the concealed heartache in his pants. "No. Whether she's engaged to you or not, I don't want to be in your family, under Gramps's control."

"That again?"

"Surprised?"

He looked at me. "Nah. Not really. I get it. If I could leave it all for you, I would."

"If there's one thing I envy about you—"

"You envy me?" He popped up.

I took a seat on the edge of the bed. Turning back to him, I said, "One thing—don't get too excited. Your parents. Your family's loyalty and love for each other. I'm not saying mine totally sucks, well, maybe my mom does. It's just different. I don't have the relationship you have with your mom, or for that matter, what Nigel has with his mom. I lost that a year ago, when Grandma died."

Zach caressed the back of my shoulder. "I'm sorry. Tate, if you speak—"

"I can't." I jumped to my feet to get away from his touch. "Please stop asking."

"Tatey, I'm home. Hewwo?" Toni's little voice yelled.

"Hey, look who's here." Zach grinned.

Then we both snapped our heads toward his *concealed heartache*, and with the sound of Toni's little voice, all was solved. Zach mouthed a Hail Mary and jogged out of the bedroom. When they saw each other, Toni smiled and yipped, and Zach put his arms out.

She ran full speed for him. "Zachy. I missed you."

He spun her around. "I missed you too, Mouse. How was your Christmas?" He put her down.

"I got Malibu Barbie!"

They were like old friends. Zach was great with Toni. She was giggling and hamming it up for him. He appeared genuinely amused.

"Tone, how was school? Any writing homework?" I asked.

Zach chuckled. "I miss the days of those handwriting sheets. Now, that's serious first grade homework."

"A wittle." Toni rolled her blue eyes.

"Okay, why don't you get it out and done before Mom and Dad get home. Then we can watch some cartoons."

"Do you know how good of a sis you have, Tone?"

"She's okay." Toni jogged off. "I'll get Barbie and show you."

Zach, the tall, dark, handsome Italian with great bed hair, didn't take his eyes off me as he took one step at a time toward me. "One day you'll forget about my gramps and choose me over fear."

CHAPTER 7

Zach

FOR THE FIRST TIME SINCE I'd been shipped to Italy, my head was in the right place. Tatum always had a way of making me see a different—usually a better—perspective. I didn't care to drink, especially if not drinking meant kissing her.

I wouldn't allow the bottle to control me anymore. God knew there were enough people in my life doing a fine job of that already.

Tatum and I sat in the living room watching TV. She kept glancing at the clock.

"Tate, you waiting for something?"

"Uh, yeah. Nigel is coming over soon."

There went my harmony. *Now, how to get rid of this guy? Of course, her dealing with my shit wasn't helping my case any.* "Do you want me to leave?"

"No, Zachy. You stay too. Nigle watches TB wif us too." Toni thought she was gonna control the situation too.

Tatum gave me those beautiful puppy dog blues. "It's probably best. I need to break it to him that you're back."

"I'm back? You mean—"

"Well, he knows you're my ex. And he knows you left town unexpectedly. I try not to talk about my feelings about you any more than I have to."

"What feelings do you have for me? Exactly?"

"Zach." She huffed and rolled those gorgeous eyes of hers. "You know I have feelings for you, but it doesn't matter. There are too many complicating factors here. I'm with Nige. I need you to respect that. Just like I'm going to respect you're engaged. You have commitments. I have other commitments."

Ouch. Tatum knew how to hit below the belt . . . that was my girl. "I don't have to like it, though."

A car pulled up and we both jerked our stares to the front door.

Toni jumped to her feet. "Nigle's here."

Now I had to deal with him. I had to keep my cool at Tatum's house. Thank God Toni was with us.

"Zach, I beg you—"

"I know. I know. Let me meet him and then I'll leave. I don't want Mom to have to deal with *her* for long."

Toni flung open the door. "Hi Nigle. Wook whose back."

Damn it, Toni.

Tatum hustled to the door. "Hi, Nige."

I just wanted to see the guy she was choosing over me, then I'd leave. I didn't want him touching my spoken for. Thankfully I trusted that Tatum wouldn't do anything with Toni here, but still.

A guy with long wavy black hair stepped up and wrapped his competitive arms around Tatum. Italian blood boiled over in seconds. He stared at me with blue eyes that I could swear told me to get out. Ha. I wasn't going anywhere. I turned away to avoid personally taking his hands off of her.

Tatum invited him inside and awkwardly led Nigel to me. "Zach, this is my boyfriend, Nigel. Nigel, this is Zach."

He wore a British decorum smile, but his jealousy rolled off him in waves. I knew, because I felt it too.

"Zach. Mate. Nice to finally meet Tatum's… ex."

Holy shit. Her Nigel was actually British? And he resembled someone, but who? I shook his hand. "Yeah, nice to meet the luckiest guy on Earth."

Tatum backhanded my shoulder. "Stop." She played coy, taking a quick glance at me.

"True."

"So, you're back in town. To stay?" Nigel asked.

Suppose he wanted to see what competition he had to deal with. A lot if he wanted her. He'd have to fight harder than I already had. And I felt confident there was no way he'd last longer than me.

"I'm back for the entire semester. I won't be moving away, just leaving from time to time."

"Moving back and forth is tough." Nigel wrapped his arm around Tatum's waist.

The waist I wanted more than my life. I wanted to break his fingers. I could have—

"Um, Zach, you're welcome to stay if you'd like," Tatum gave me *the face*. The *please stop* face.

"Uh, thanks, but I gotta go. Anyway. Nice to meet you, Nigel. Tate, see you in the morning?"

Toni came running over and hugged my legs. "Bye, Zachy. See you tomorrow. Nigle, you stay and watch TB with me."

Nigel was a nice guy because if I were in his shoes, I would make it clear the ex wasn't welcomed back.

"Sure, Toni. Let's watch *Duck Tales*," Nigel said.

"I'm going to walk him out. Save me a seat." Tatum stretched up on her tiptoes and laid a kiss on Nigel's cheek.

Toni took Nigel's hand and led him to the couch.

Outside, I took my time unlocking the car door. Tatum stood next to me. "Hey. Take it easy. I have a lot of explaining to do once I get back in there. Be happy he didn't slug you."

The woman made my heart—and other things—ache. "Baby . . . I mean, Tate. You read my mind. Because if the shoe were on the other foot, I would have slugged him."

"Call me if you need anything." She stared up at me. "I can tell your eyes are looking a lot better. You don't have anything on you, so be ready for when the cravings begin."

I slid my hand on that perfect waist. "Don't let him touch you again." I gave her a kiss on the cheek. "I'll have a plan, don't worry. *Ti amo così tanto*, Tatum."

"Zach, we just talked about this . . . it can't be that way."

Like hell.

"Call if you need anything," she said again.

"Don't put it like that . . . you'll get a call." She was getting a call no matter what. I'd seen how she reacted when Nigel talked, but she'd reacted the same to me just now when I spoke Italian. And he had no clue how she'd reacted to me in her bed.

She shook her head and waved as she walked away. "Bye, Zach. Night."

God help me. She was going back in there with him . . . don't drink, you can do this!

Why a British guy? Girls loved listening to the Brits talk.

I got in my car and dialed my mom to let her know I was on my way, but my mom didn't answer. "Who is this?" I asked.

"Zacharia Bertano, I your fidanzato!" Mariacella laughed.

"Where's my mother?" Hearing Mariacella laugh about my life going down the shit drain felt like she stabbed me in the gut, gave a solid twist and then slowly pulled the knife out.

"You could ask me how I doing. When you coming home? I miss you."

I considered how upset Tatum would be at me for going against my word and drinking. Dealing with this tramp was going to kill me. But if I were to break my word, Tatum would never forgive me. I had to redirect my anger. Because right then I was pretty angry my life was so shitty.

I sucked in a deep breath and counted to five. "Mariacella, love, could you be so kind to put my mother on the phone? I'm heading home now."

"Oh, you soo romantic. I get ready for you. Here's your mother, she was in the bathroom."

The last thing I wanted to touch was Mariacella, especially since I still had Tatum all over me.

The phone shuffled. "Zach? Is everything okay? And Mariacella, I've asked you to please not answer my phone."

"Mom, I'm on my way home."

"How did it go?"

"It went fine. I can't live without her. She's the one." I continued to tell my mom about some of what happened and how there was no way Tatum would speak for me anytime soon. "Then her little sister showed up."

"Toni?"

"Yeah. Mom, she's so cute. Watching Tatum with her sister, I know she'll be an excellent mom one day."

"Zacharia, that makes me so happy."

"Well, don't get too happy. Her boyfriend showed up, Nigel."

"Oh dear . . . you went face to face? Please Zacharia, tell me you didn't do anything."

"Give me some credit."

"I won't while you're drinking."

"I told you, Tate poured it all out. And trust me, seeing how hurt Tate was because of my drinking, I really don't have the desire to drink anymore."

"I hope so."

"Anyhow, he's British and it kills me to say . . . good-looking. And I could see why Tate went gaga. She's just infatuated with him, because I know she's not in love with him. She's in love with me, it's just Gramps scares her more."

"You could be right about the infatuation. I think Tatum is the kind of girl who needs to come to terms, her terms, and then she'll agree. She's stubborn, so you'll have to be patient. Let's just see how things play out for now." The phone shuffled again. "Zach?" Mom whispered. "She's waiting for you in your room. Please don't drink tonight. Come straight home. She leaves in a month. Then you'll have Tate until June."

I never meant to worry my mom. She was the second most important woman in my life. "I'll be there in five minutes."

CHAPTER 8

Tatum

I STEPPED INTO THE LIVING ROOM. Nigel didn't say a word while he stared at me. He was evaluating my reaction to him.

"Um, Nige . . . can you come in my bedroom for a minute? Toni, we need to talk in private. Be right back."

He patted Toni's leg. "Tell me what happens to the Ducks when I get back."

"Okay, Nigle. Don't be wong."

In my bedroom I chose to pace the floor, and Nigel took a seat on the wood frame of my waterbed. "I can only imagine what you're thinking. And I can't say I blame you. But it's not as it looks."

"Tatum, he's back? What does that mean for us?"

Nigel's eyes drooped. He was worried. I braced my hands on his big shoulders. "Zach is back in town, nothing more. He left me high and dry. Just because he's back in St. Louis for the semester doesn't mean I'm running back to him. I'm your girlfriend. You'll learn when I make a commitment, I keep it." Whether it killed me or not. This was the right decision. The safe decision. I had to be honest with myself: I cared deeply for Zach, but there were advantages to being with Nigel.

"Tatum, I was here for ten seconds and could feel the heat in the room between you two. The way he looked at you, he's still in love with you."

"I can't speak for him and his feelings, but trust me, you have nothing to worry about." It would take more than heat to get me to agree to be in Gramps's Mob family.

Nigel put his arms around me. "But are you still in love with him? Blimey, Tate . . . just be honest. I won't stand in your way. If you want to be with him, just say it."

My heart shouted louder than Sam Kinison in frustration. Nigel didn't believe I wasn't in love with Zach anymore. He was right, I would always love Zach, but I'm not in love with him because being in love with Zach also meant loving the Mob too. I'd die before I let that happen.

"Nigel, I'm your girlfriend and I'm in love with you. Only you."

He popped up to his feet and cradled my body in his, kissing my lips. My lips weren't enough. He kissed along my neck line and back up to my ear. His breath on my skin sent a shiver through my body.

He whispered, "I want you to be honest with me. So I'm going to be honest with you; I love you, m'lady."

I held my mouth against Nigel's ear. "I love you too. Don't worry."

He held my face and kissed my lips. The thought of two men ran across my mind. One I was madly in love with. And one I used to be in love with. And I was where I needed to be.

The next morning, Zach was at my locker again. This was different, though. His eyes weren't bloodshot, they were clear.

"Zach, I can't tell you how happy I am you kept your word."

"It's all about redirecting bad energy!"

I wanted to laugh at him, but didn't. "Good. Good to hear you actually listened."

If he only knew I had no clue what I was talking about, he wouldn't have put so much faith in what I said. It seemed to be working; that was all that mattered.

He bent down to my face. "I respect and love you. You're worth everything."

Okay, time to shut him out. He was saying the right things, and he knew it.

"Hey, what's going on, you two?" Diane walked up. She had impeccable timing.

"Nothing, heading to class. You coming?"

"Sure am. Don't you find it weird, Tate, that we have, like, most of our classes together this semester?" Diane shoved her oversized black plastic frames up her nose.

"I've thought about that too. Zach? Your thoughts?"

The three of us had almost every hour together. He'd definitely done something to make that happen. What, though? No clue, but something.

"Totally weird." Zach didn't give us the time of day. He stared straight ahead.

Saturday, January 20, 1990

I had gotten home from work and had to hurry to be ready before Nigel picked me up. Of course that meant the phone rang and my mom was calling for me to pick up.

"Hello?" I didn't mean to sound so out of breath.

"Tate. It's Zach."

I did not need to deal with Zach's bullshit. He had "company," and he needed to focus on her. Besides, I needed the constant contact to end. "Yeah. Whatchya need?"

"I just wanted to let you know I'm thinking about you."

"Why? Aren't you busy with your fidanzato?"

"Tatum, you're upset . . . what's going on?"

"You must be drinking again. Maybe my problem is your constantly calling me even though she's still here. In your house. Maybe that's what's wrong."

"I know. She leaves in two weeks. Look . . . I don't want to fight. I just wanted to let you know that I'm thinking about you because I know what today is."

"And that is?"

"Tatum, this is the day your grandma passed away. I know it's not easy for you."

Sword inserted and pulled out. "I'm fine. Don't worry about me. But thanks for remembering." Whether he still had Mariacella with him or not, it was nice of him to remember what today meant to me.

"Zach, I gotta go. Nigel should be here soon."

"Okay, but call if you need an ear. I'm always here for you, Tate."

"Thanks a lot. Have a good weekend, Zach." I hung up. The sad thing is, he meant it, but nothing more. Because if Gramps interfered again, Zach wouldn't be allowed to be there for me.

I took a deep breath and had to let all of the confusing emotions out. That always made me feel better. Grandma always encouraged meditation. Nothing cleared my mind more.

I wanted to avoid Nigel having to come inside and talk to my parents or deal with Toni for another cartoon sitting, so I ran outside when I heard him pull up.

"Hey, I was coming in to get you."

"No need. I'm here. You ready?" I hopped in the passenger seat.

Nigel drove off with a smile on his face. "I was thinking dinner before we meet up with the others, but one stop first."

"Sure."

It wasn't until Nigel pulled into the cemetery that I felt it necessary to question our agenda. "Uhh . . . Nigel?"

He patted my knee. "I know what today is."

"You do? How?"

"You told me on New Year's Eve. I can remember dates well. Hope this is okay?"

"Sure it is. But I don't have any flowers or anything. Darn . . . if I knew—"

"Gotchya covered." Nigel reached in the backseat and grabbed a silk flower arrangement. The red roses and pink carnations with greenery were perfect for their grave.

Judging by the erratic pulsating of my heart, it would soon explode. Nigel knew how to touch my soul. My eyes were heavy. One blink and a tear would escape. I was visiting my grandma. It'd been a whole year since I had seen her. Of course, I wasn't able to "see" her. But the idea of being near made my heart flutter with the vibrations of hummingbirds.

Not to compare Nigel to Zach, but while a phone call was very sweet, taking me to my grandmother's grave was another ballpark.

"Nigel, I don't know what to say. No one has ever done this for me before."

He pulled over and looked at me, smiling, pearly whites exposed. "Say nothing. Come on, you'll have to lead the way."

Nigel got out of the car and held my hand while I walked him to the Virgin Mary statue where Grandma had had to be buried.

With Nigel at my side, I placed the flowers at my grandparents' headstone. "Grandma? Grandpa? This is Nigel, my boyfriend." I was so glad to be there, but it hit me harder with the reality of what I'd lost lying in front of me.

Nigel squeezed me to his side. My heart wouldn't slow. "Nigel, this is so incredibly sweet of you. Thank you. I'm sure my grandparents are happy for the visit."

"Of course, but don't you come here often?"

"No. Never. It's just too far to walk. And my parents never come here."

"Really? That's sad. If my dad were buried in the US, we would visit weekly."

"So imagine how much this means to me."

Inches from his face, I hoisted up on my tiptoes. Nigel pulled me up to his warm lips for a tender kiss. It was cold outside in the mid-January evening, but I didn't feel the brisk breeze with Nigel wrapped around me.

"Happy New Year, Grandma and Grandpa. Love you." I turned my attention to the graveyard. The trees were bare, dormant. The grass was yellow-brown. It was depressing. Other headstones were decorated from Christmas. Thanks to Nigel, my grandparents weren't left out of the only color among the lost. Maybe it wasn't the most romantic place to take your date, but I wasn't a typical date. And what I loved more was that Nigel understood that about me.

Not that there was any doubt, but his is more validation I'm where I should be.

I smiled up at Nigel to give him the go-ahead, and he led me back to the car.

On the drive to the restaurant, a headache wanted to ruin my night. So many thoughts were going through my mind about the benefits of dating Nigel over Zach. Nigel knew what it was like to lose someone who meant the world to you. We had that in common.

After dinner, we met up with Scotty, Val, and a few of his other friends. While others played games or made out behind a closed door, Nigel and I snuggled up at the stone fireplace in the sixties-style living room with a dropped floor. Being wrapped in a faux fur throw and Nigel's arms said I was home.

"Thanks again for taking me to see Grandma and Grandpa tonight. It was a pleasant surprise."

"Hey, no prob. I'll take you weekly if you want. Or whenever you want to visit them. Just because you don't have a car and your parents don't go shouldn't mean you can't."

Nigel knew exactly what to say to me. "Thanks."

"Not to change the subject, but I have a question. I know we have a few months, but I was thinking about Prom."

"Prom? Isn't Prom in May?"

"Yeah. But there's a lot coming up this semester. I'm going to England for spring break."

"England?"

"Yeah, Lester, my stepdad, has business there, and he's taking Bren and me with him. We haven't been back for a few years, and this is our opportunity."

So the one week I could be with him without school interfering, he wouldn't even be in the country. Maybe it was selfish, but darn. "Sounds dreamy."

"Then my Prom is Saturday, May fifth. Would you go with me?"

"You really have a thing for planning ahead." Nigel's smile faded. "Of course I'll go with you to Prom."

With my back to his chest, he cradled his arms around me and kissed the side of my ear. "Love you, Tatum." Nigel tugged at my earlobe with his lips.

The tug meant more than acceptance, it meant *please love me as much as I love you*. If not more. "Love you too, Nige."

"I'm just going to say it." Nigel kept his mouth at my ear. "I know you still love him, and it sucks, but I appreciate you giving us a solid try."

I spun around in between his legs and landed inches from his face. "Why would you say that, Nigel? No matter what Zach and I had, it would never work between us. Never. There's things you get and he doesn't. Like earlier . . . he called me, didn't offer to take me to the cemetery. And look, I hate comparing or judging, it's not fair to either. He has chaos going on in his life right now, but it doesn't change the fact there's certain things I can't let go about him. With you, I don't have to change. Neither you nor your family expect something else from me. I will always care about him. But it will never ever work. You and I have what's more important to me, and that I would never have with him. Never. You're it."

Nigel grabbed me and took my lips in a fierce kiss. With his big hands, he pulled my body against his. I felt safe. Wanted. And loved. Yes. Nigel was my safe, secure boyfriend. And there was nothing wrong with that. Nothing.

I combed my hands through the soft waves of his hair. Nigel had music on quietly in the background that I noticed without us talking. The warmth from the crackling fireplace danced across my back. I wrapped my legs around him, and Nigel slid his hands underneath me. We fit.

I could have it all with Nigel, and more.

CHAPTER 9

Zach

Friday, February 2, 1990

AFTER A MONTH OF HAVING Mariacella sleep in my house, my sentence was coming to an end. It all came down to one more night, then the bitch was gone.

Once Mariacella got on her plane the next morning, I could focus on Tatum and getting rid of Nigel. I had a long way to go, but with the Italian Princess out of my way, I wouldn't have to deal with Tatum giving me the look—the one that said, *You have no right giving me crap about kissing Nigel when your fiancée is sleeping in your house.*

But the way Tatum would roll her eyes when she said that to me . . . made it all okay.

"Zacharia? Zacharia?"

Mariacella's voice was worse than a chair leg scraping on the ceramic floor. I took a deep breath and turned my gaze up to hers. "Sorry, what?"

"What are you ordering to eat? Shall we get a bottle of wine?"

"If you want, Mariacella. But I'm not drinking. Remember?" I'd taken her to Gramps's place for two reasons. So she could drink if she wanted and so Gramps could see me making an "effort" with my betrothed.

"You don't drink anymore. You no fun."

She was the most unsupportive person. I glanced at my watch. Eleven more hours and she would be gone. I could make it.

The new waiter, Michael, came over and it didn't take an observant person to notice Mariacella eyeing the young guy like he was a Chippendale stripper. I say "young," but he was older than us. The typical waiter in Bertano's averaged forty years old, and Michael was twenty-five.

"Zach? Missus? Are you ready to order drinks?"

Mariacella wiggled her ass and pressed her chest over the edge of the table. "Oh, Michael, we love drinks."

I lost my appetite.

"Zach, a bottle?" Mariacella asked.

"Michael, whatever my missus would like. It's her last night here. We must show her real Bertano hospitality. What wine would fit the bill?" I felt violated by my own words. Hopefully Mariacella believed the filth I'd just fed her.

"I would recommend Bruno Giacosa's Barolo Riserva Falletto."

Mariacella took a deep breath, puffing her chest out, and grinned at me. She knew that was over a hundred bucks a bottle, and she would have two. Maybe Gramps would consider this making an effort, though.

"That sounds perfect. Thanks, Michael," I said.

"Sir." Michael nodded and walked away.

"Oh Zacharia, I going to miss you. You come visit me over spring break?"

"Sorry, I can't. Working. This summer?"

"Uhh, that's so long from now," Mariacella whined. She took her hand across the table to find mine. "You take me dancing tonight? Something? I want to stay out and be close to you one last time."

I scanned the restaurant's dining room, not looking at her. "Sure, for a bit." Great. What other torture would I have to endure before she left?

Michael served the wine and took our order. I wanted to call Tatum before she went out with Nigel for the night. "I'll be right back. If he serves us, go ahead and start without me."

I hustled into the men's lounge and checked the stalls for privacy. I was alone. I flipped my mobile and dialed Tatum.

"Hello?"

The moment I heard her voice, the anger and bitterness evaporated.

"Tate, it's me. When are you leaving?"

"Zacharia Bertano."

God, she kills me, the way she says my name goes right to my groin. It's so hot.

"I don't question your evening plans with your fidanzato, so don't you ask me about mine with my boyfriend." She took a deep breath. "Soon. Why?"

"I was just thinking about you, and wishing you'd be careful. So be careful tonight."

She laughed. "Okay. What does that mean? I'm confused . . . all I'm doing is working, and Nigel's kind enough to drive me back and forth."

"Nothing. Just . . . I love you."

"Okay, look . . . are you drinking again, cause Zach . . . I swear . . . don't you dare call me when you're drunk."

"I'm not drunk."

"Drinking?"

"Zaaach?" Tatum dragged my name out.

"Look, she leaves in the morning, call this a celebratory toast to her departure."

"Whatever. Hold on . . . *Coming.* Zach, I gotta go. Nigel just pulled up." I could hear the excitement in her voice.

I needed that drink. "I'll call you after she leaves tomorrow."

"Sure. Goodnight." Tatum hung up, not waiting for me to respond.

The longer Mariacella was living with me, the closer Tatum grew to Nigel. Couldn't say I blamed her. My fidanzato was a deal breaker for most, especially me.

I snapped my mobile shut and rejoined Mariacella at the table.

By the look of her eyes, she'd had a glass already.

"Here. I poured you one, drink with me." Mariacella held her glass up.

It wouldn't kill me to play along. I picked up my glass and put it next to hers. "To my fidanzato. May she have a safe trip back home and may we make our families happy in the end."

"Salute." She tapped against my glass.

That was good wine. *Better be for the price Gramps paid.*

Mariacella and I rarely had conversations. Nothing more than *What do you want? Where are you taking me?* and *Let's get drunk.* She wasn't much of a deep thinker. Maybe for some guys that was perfect. For me, it reminded me how much I loved Tatum.

Over the course of dinner, I milked my one glass of wine but felt completely drunk. How did one glass of wine have that kind of effect on me? After four or five glasses, sure, but not one. I did my best not to slur or sway, but the room was out of focus and it was difficult to keep anything straight.

"Zacharia, let's leave."

"Yeah. Sorry, I can't go dancing, Mariacella. Can you drive us? Or shall I call Tyler?"

"I happy to drive you, my love."

I put the keys on the table, not trusting myself to put them in her hand.

Michael came back over. "Zach, sir? You all right?"

"Michael, what proof was that wine?"

"Thirteen percent, Sir."

"My head." I rested my forehead in the palm of my hands. "It's just . . . one glass has never hit me like this."

"You no worry, Michael. I drive him. Tell Mr. Bertano grazie for me."

Michael said nothing, but remained at my side.

"It's okay. The missus is driving me. Thanks, Mike. Catch ya next time."

"If you're sure? I'll call Catalina to let her know."

"He is fine. I can take care of my man myself," Mariacella snapped.

I waved my hand and Michael walked off. "He's just trying to help. He means nothing by it, Maria."

She stepped up to me and caressed the side of my cheek. "I like when you call me Maria."

"Good. I like it more anyway. Can we go now?"

Mariacella drove us toward home, but then she turned off onto Missouri Bottom Road—a dark road that ran along the Missouri River. "Maria? You passed our turn."

It was dark and secluded. Few people traveled this road because it was unlit and so close to the river's edge. It was scary for some.

She pulled off the road into a gravel area, parked and turned the ignition off. "I want us to be alone. You mother is always listening to us. I want you all to myself without her prying eyes."

I reclined my seat back, not feeling well. I'd never been so drunk. And the car began spinning. My blurred vision and slurred speech was embarrassing. I couldn't see straight.

"Maria, just take me home. I'm tired and need to go to bed."

"I take you to bed, Zacharia. Stay back. I make you feel better."

She crawled on top of me. Oomph. "What are you doing?"

"Please. Just this once before I leave."

I felt weak. Weak enough to not be able to stop her from unzipping my pants. "Maria, stop. Not here."

"Just relax, Zacharia. Listen to my voice," Mariacella whispered. "I love you. I make you happy. Close your eyes. No one is here but us."

She shoved my chest and forced me to recline. I was so tired, and the darkness didn't help matters. I wanted to sleep.

"I love you, Zach. No matter what happens."
Tatum?

I glanced down between my legs and saw Tatum's face. She smiled up at me. "Relax."

Tatum was the last person I wanted to argue with. She made it easy to do what she requested with the pleasure she propelled through my body. She was awesome. I grabbed the sides of her head and tangled her hair between my fingers. "I love you so much, baby."

I wanted this woman forever. She was the only thing in life that made me happy.

The sound of a foghorn blasted through my ears. I jumped up and my head almost exploded from the pressure. What the hell? I held my head and blinked my eyes to focus with the light pouring in the car. Finally, my sight came back. A thin layer of frost was on the front and back windshields. I could see my own breath. Damn, it was cold.

I turned and found a kink in my back. I glanced around to get my bearings. Mariacella and I were in the backseat of my car. Both of us were naked, but we had blankets draped over us. What happened? I prayed we didn't do what I feared. My car was parked in a gravel pull-off down by the river. A huge barge was floating past us. Not a good place to be for long.

I reached over and shook Mariacella. "Wake up. Did you drive us down here?"

I couldn't remember anything after the restaurant. I'd called Tatum, then had a glass of wine with dinner and then talked to Michael about letting Mariacella take my keys. That was the last of my memory.

I shook her again. "Your flight leaves in three hours. We have to go."

She moaned and groaned. I tossed her clothes at her and hastily pulled on my pants. There didn't seem to be a condom anywhere. Not sure why I was so drunk from one glass of wine. Unless I had more and didn't remember.

Over now. Whatever happened, happened. Maybe I didn't want to remember what took place. My focus was getting her things from my house before I drove her ass to the airport.

When we walked into my parents' house fifteen minutes later, Mom and Dad sat at the kitchen island, drinking coffee and giving me the look of disappointment.

Mariacella continued past them. "I be ready soon, love." She went into her bedroom and slammed the door shut.

I stepped up to the coffee pot and poured. "Don't ask, because I honestly have no clue." After splashing in a dash of sugar and milk, I turned around to face them.

"Zach, Michael called me. He was worried and said you looked drunk off your ass. I thought you promised the German not to drink."

It was cute how my mother insisted on not saying Tatum's name while Mariacella was at the house. "I had a glass of wine. One. I don't know why it hit me like that."

Dad turned back to the bedroom hall before stepping up to me. "We think she probably drugged you. Where did you wake up?"

"In the car. On Mo Bottom Rd. Pulled off to the side."

My parents looked at each other. "Did you two . . ."

I loved my parents, but wasn't sure why they were so comfortable with my sexual relations. "I don't know. Maybe."

"Oh my God, Zach. Do not tell me you didn't use—"

"I don't know because I don't know what I did. Wait." Tatum. I remembered Tatum and I . . . oh no . . .

"What? What is it?" My mom sounded panicked.

"I remember being in the passenger seat and Tatum down my . . . Never mind."

"Jesus, Nicola. What did she use on him if he was hallucinating?"

"Suppose she could have given him some kind of mushroom extract or even LSD. Lots of things."

My stomach churned. *If that wasn't Tatum . . . of course it wasn't Tatum. Idiot. That was Mariacella. Oh my God. What did I do?*

I heard a whimper. I snapped out of it and noticed Mom wiping her eyes and Dad comforting her.

"Mom? What is it?"

"I had a dream last night. I thought it was Tatum, but now I think it may have been Mariacella."

"Okay. A dream about what? Why are you crying?"

"A girl we know was pregnant."

"Who, Mom?" I became panicked.

"I don't know. A girl."

My world caved in around me and I was smothering. The possibility of getting the wedding called off. The idea of being with Tatum, forever. Getting rid of

Mariacella for good . . . all gone. Poof.

A pair of hands had hold of my shoulders and was shaking me. "Zach? Snap out of it. We need to get her to the airport. I want her gone. Move now. Go freshen up. Get her packed, we leave in ten minutes. Go." Dad was out of patience.

If I did it with Mariacella, and it looked like I did, and if she was pregnant, I was done for. My life would be over. I couldn't leave a Bertano baby. I would have to marry her and help raise my child. She did this on purpose. She knew the Bertano rules. We never turn our backs on our own. Never.

CHAPTER 10

Zach

Saturday, February 3, 1990

A T THE AIRPORT, MY PARENTS stayed back while I continued to the gate with Mariacella. The airline called for pre-boarders.

Mariacella dropped her bag and threw her arms around my neck. "Zacharia, I miss you. I call you when I get in tonight."

Just a minute longer. "Sure. You do that. Get some rest too."

"You so thoughtful." She kissed my lips.

I patted her back and pulled away. "They're boarding first class, you better get settled."

"You come see me soon. Spring break?"

She was leaving. It wasn't the time to argue with her. "Call me when you land."

Mariacella grabbed her bag and walked off, blowing me a kiss. I half waved and watched my nightmare walk onto the gangway. The moment she stepped out of sight, the weight of the Colosseum was lifted off my chest. I'd survived. For now.

I found my parents by the security screening.

"She's gone?" Dad asked.

"Yeah. I'm so happy I could scream."

My parents flanked me on our walk back to the car.

"Now, the task is to catch her screwing up," Mom said.

"Or how about just her screwing someone else."

My parents looked at me. "But let her be the one cheating," Dad remarked.

"What does that mean?"

Mom patted my shoulder. "Calm down, Zach. It means . . . don't touch Tatum. No matter what happens with her and Nigel."

"Look. Tate is even more infatuated with the Brit. This month has killed any chance I had when we first got back. If anything happens, it won't be for a while."

"Sorry to say, but good. Keep it that way. At least until we catch Mariacella doing something we can use to call off this wedding," Dad said.

When we got back home, I ran to my room to call Tatum. Damage control began now.

"Tate? It's me. Can you talk?"

"For a minute. I have to work tonight. I'm not a happy camper. I told my mom about them putting me on both Friday and Saturday nights . . . it's my whole darn weekend."

"Well, maybe this will make you feel better."

"I won the lottery and don't have to work?"

Her sarcasm was cute, because if she would speak for me she wouldn't have to work. Of course it also made me a little happy that it meant she wasn't with Nigel, falling in love with him even more. I gave the guy credit, he was better than I expected.

"Guess who left?"

"Elvis."

"Funny, Tatum. Funny. No, the Italian princess."

"Ohh." was all she said.

"I'm free, Tate!"

"Is the wedding called off?" Her tone was sharp.

"Not yet. First things first. Look . . . this isn't going to happen over—"

"Yeah, and I can't and won't put my life on hold for you. You are not *free*. Just let it go. *We* will never happen."

"No. It will. Now listen—"

"No. You listen. I will never be in Gramps's family. The End."

"This isn't over."

"The hell it isn't. Just face the music, Zach. No matter what *was* between us, it's over. I'm in love with Nigel. Do you hear me? I love Nigel. Just stay with *her* and get your vineyard. I'm being honest . . . it sounds great. If we were meant to be together, life wouldn't make it so hard for that to happen. So just accept the way things are. I gotta go. I hate this stupid job."

A jolt of anger shot through me. There were only a few things in life that made me mad, but one of them was Tatum's inability to believe in people. She had no clue what she was talking about. I wanted to strangle her and insist this could work. The woman had no patience. I took a deep breath and swiped the back of my hand across my forehead. "I understand. I'll talk to you tomorrow, unless you need a ride home after work?"

She laughed. "Ha! Nice try, Zacharia."

"Is Nigel getting you then?"

"Yes. Don't start."

"I'm not. Call if you need anything, if something changes."

"Night, Zach."

I clicked the receiver and waited for the dial tone to call Tyler.

He picked up on the first ring. "Yes?"

"Tyler, we need to talk."

"I take it Princess is flying right now?"

"Princess is long gone. So, now we need to get this wedding called off. But . . . I want her dad's vineyard too."

"Getting the wedding called off is easy. She's bound to screw up. But his vineyard . . . you are an eager Bertano. No wonder Gramps wants you to take over—"

"Yeah. Yeah. Yeah. Now, can you get your spoken for on the line with us?"

"Hold on." There was a click and Tyler was gone.

A few minutes later and after another click, Tyler and his spoken for, Bonita, said hello.

With more people in my court I felt a sense of victory. This would work. "Thanks for offering to help me, Bonita. I appreciate it."

"Sure. I hate Mariacella. Talk about someone who thinks she's God's gift—"

Tyler cut in. "Now, are you sure you want to do this, hon? Staying close to Mariacella can be dangerous. If you get caught—"

"Tyler? Don't worry. I can do this. Zach has the hard part. When we catch her in the act, she'll want to kill you, Zach."

"I know, but that's why I need a Plan B. Because when that time comes, all hell will break loose and the princess will be exposed. Just be careful. She's not to be trusted."

Bonita chuckled. "Don't worry your heads off, I've got this. Besides, like Catalina told me . . . I need to step it up."

"What do you mean? When did you speak with my mom, and what did she say?"

Bonita sighed. "Never mind. Just if I want to be Lead here in Italy, I better start carrying my weight."

"Zach, didn't your mom mention her visit to Bonita?" Tyler asked.

My mom meant well, but I didn't need her to piss anyone off before they agreed to help me. "Obviously not. Hmm, not sure what's going on there."

"Isn't it clear, Zach?" Tyler's voice carried heat. "Cat is planning on you and Tatum taking over in Italy. Unless Bonita and I prove ourselves, we lose *my* dad's spot."

Why would my mother do something like that? She knew that whether Tatum and I ended up together or not, there was no way we were living in Italy doing the family's work. Unless . . . I did get the Davides' vineyard. "I assure you, you and Bonita can have Italy. I have no desire to be there, and I'm sure Tatum wouldn't either. Shall I put that in writing?"

Tyler exhaled. "No. Sorry. It just rubbed me the wrong way. I know you and Tate wouldn't bump us."

"As my dear German would say, *no worries*. Keep Italy. So are we on track for burying my fidanzato?"

"As soon as possible, Zach," Bonita eagerly said.

"You can count on us," Tyler sighed.

"I really appreciate that. I thank you and so does Tatum . . . she just doesn't know it yet!"

CHAPTER 11

Tatum

Monday, February 5, 1990

I WAS SITTING AT OUR LUNCH table with the usual suspects, but this semester Di was added. She was always entertaining. With the mysterious identical schedules, we were on the same lunch break. I didn't complain.

At least, I didn't until Zach wouldn't shut up about his Italian princess being back across the pond.

"Okay, we know she's gone. We know you're thrilled. But we don't need to hear any more about how annoying she is. We know!" The last words came out a little louder than I meant.

"Changing the subject," Di jumped in, "Valentine's Day is coming up and I have some news."

I stopped chopping up my salad. Di almost never had news.

Di didn't look at anyone in particular. "Tommy asked me to dinner on Valentine's Day. And I said yes!"

Andi and I simultaneously shrieked.

I tossed my arms around her. "Di, I'm so happy for you." She had been single for too long.

"So how is the annoying ass?" Andi smirked and then looked away.

Matt didn't take his eyes off her.

If Matt ever knew what Andi did New Year's Eve at Nigel's house, she would be in deep trouble. Participating in a game of Streaking in the Park and then letting another guy carry her topless body back to Nigel's house . . . hearing about that would set Matt off. Couldn't blame him there. But Andi's secret was safe with Di and me.

"The annoying ass is well. It seems as if he and Jessie worked out whatever they were fighting over at New Year's Eve, which is good."

They were fighting over Di and her attention, and she knew that.

"Well, good. Nigel hasn't said anything, but I suppose those guys are close-lipped about stuff like that."

"Tate?" Zach sat up. "Are you doing anything for Cupid's Day?"

"I am."

"He's taking you out?"

"Yeah."

Zach took a deep breath, I could see his shoulders raise and fall with a neck roll.

"Don't you get all huffy about this, Zacharia. Are you still engaged?"

Zach said a big fat nothing.

"I thought so. You have no right getting jealous."

Matt sat there saying nothing, but for a not-so-obvious head shake.

Andi talked about their plans for Valentine's Day,

and Zach's posture turned more intense. Whether the dirty bastard was still engaged to that tramp or not, I felt bad for him.

I patted his shoulder. "I'm free this coming Sunday, you wanna do lunch at the mall?" *Hope this doesn't come back and bite me in the ass.*

His eyes brightened with a sparkle. "What time shall I pick you up?"

"Noon."

"You guys are impossible." Andi shook her head.

I couldn't stand to see him hurt. His family sucked, but he couldn't help the situation they put him in. Kicking a dog when it was down wasn't my style. Unless he annoyed me.

The Sunday before Valentine's Day, Zach and I were walking the mall, not hand in hand. Once we'd gotten there and gone inside, it was weird enough between us. Going to the mall with Nigel was a weekly outing. I wasn't doing anything wrong, but my conscience nagged me worse than my mom. What made it even worse for me, and I was sure for Zach too, was that going to the mall was something we used to do as a couple too, before he left me for Italy without a word.

It was a typical Sunday afternoon. The sounds of children playing echoed off the white speckled ceramic floors, polished with a mirrored shine, and through the mall's oversized potted landscaping.

"Tate, if you see anything you want, let me know."

"I'm not letting you buy me anything. Don't be silly."

We walked passed the Dillard's storefront displays. There was the cutest outfit in the window. I loved shopping, but wasn't creative enough to put outfits together. It was best to see an ensemble on a mannequin first, and then purchase that particular outfit.

"I see how you're looking at the windows. Just go try something on."

"I'm fine." We kept walking. "I don't mean to upset you, but do you have any plans at all for Wednesday?"

"No. You're busy."

"Zach, I know you have the princess situation, but if you can get rid of that, maybe it's time you moved on—"

"I am not talking to you about that, Tate."

"Well, I'm putting my heart on my sleeve."

"Ha . . . you?"

"Zach." At least I made him smile. "Seriously. Nigel and I are in lo—"

"And I'm not talking about that."

"Okay, fine. But will you—"

"Shit."

"Fine. Be impossible." I noticed Zach's eyes narrowed in from his relatively content face. I turned toward the mall and noticed Nigel and Tommy heading in our direction.

"Nigel!" I yipped and ran for his arms.

He grabbed a hold and spun me around, kissing my face. "M'lady."

We kissed each other and he put me down. I adjusted my clothes. "Nigel. What are you doing here?"

He shoved a Famous-Barr bag behind his back. "Nothing. I was just about to ask you the same thing."

"Oh . . . just hanging out." I turned back.

Zach stepped up with his hand out. "Nigel."

The boys played nice and shook hands.

Nigel glanced at Tommy. "Zach, this is my mate, Tommy."

Tommy and Zach exchanged pleasantries. Zach stood close to me.

Nigel glanced back and forth between me and Zach.

It became more awkward than a hung jury meeting with a defendant in the lobby. "So, um, Nige—"

"Tate, can I talk to you for a minute?" Nigel took my hand and pulled me far enough away so Tommy and Zach wouldn't hear our whispers. "What the hell, Tate? Out with Zach? Shopping?"

Crap. I knew he wouldn't understand, which was exactly why I hadn't told him. "Look, he's alone. I wanted to be a good friend to him."

"Sweetheart." Nigel placed his hand on my cheek. "When are you going to see he's not so lonely? He loves you."

"Nigel, not here. Please?"

"'Kay. You continue to play your charade with him, but if he lays a hand on you—"

"I've said before, I don't take to threats easily. Look, let's not fight."

"We won't fight. Just don't let him touch you."

"I don't."

Nigel wrapped his football-sized hand behind my back and pulled. "I love you, m'lady."

The ass knew my knees went weak when he talked to me like that. "Love you too."

He pulled me up to his mouth and gave me something to remember him by.

Nigel stepped back and grinned. He knew exactly what he was doing, and without question it made me want to sign the marriage license. The sad fact was, I could never have Zach without all of the baggage that went with him. Nigel didn't have any. We were better suited for each other. Zach had to understand that.

Nigel took my hand and walked me back over to the guys, who'd started their own casual conversation.

"Tommy, you ready?"

"If you are."

Nigel angled his body to Zach's and put his hand out. "Mate."

Then Nigel moved over to me and wrapped his arms around my body while showing who had full access to my lips. Boys and their testosterone crap. Of course, if the shoe were on the other foot and a girl was with Nigel, I'd have done the same thing. Maybe worse.

By time the tingle ran its course through my body, Nigel and Tommy had walked off.

Zach took a few deep breaths and brought me back to the here and now. "Yes? What?"

He didn't look at me. "Nothing. Just one day, he'll know what it feels like."

Wednesday, February 14, 1990

Nigel didn't take me to a restaurant for Valentine's Day. He and his mom prepared a meal for us at his dad's house. Mrs. Marshall left once she put dinner on the table.

"Nigel and Tatum, I'll do dishes tomorrow. Just leave them, but lock the door on your way out."

"Thanks, Mrs. Marshall. Happy Valentine's Day."

She returned the sentiment, waved, and walked out through the garage.

Nigel and I sat at his large dining room table. Fine china sparkled under the dimmed chandelier and the two taper candles glowed.

"Dig in," Nigel said.

This was the second meal Mrs. Marshall had prepared for us, and it was nice she didn't force anything but fish on me. "This looks great. Your mom is so sweet to do this. Isn't Lester taking her out tonight?"

"He's traveling, so when he gets back he's taking her out. She's been complaining all day."

Couldn't say I blamed her. "The restaurants won't be as crowded, though."

"True. She doesn't look at it that way."

Of course she didn't. I wouldn't have either.

"Tate, can I bring something up without you getting upset?"

"Of course." Was I that much of an open book with my feelings?

"Could you tell me ahead of time when you're doing something with Zach? Not that this is the reason, but it didn't look good when Tommy noticed I didn't know you were out with the Italian."

"Uh, 'the Italian'?" Nigel's jealousy was getting worse. I wasn't sure how to handle it because I couldn't fault him, for I once had been in love with Zach. I needed to be stronger and not worry so much about Zach and his loneliness.

"Zach."

Why was he reluctant to even say Zach's name? "Nige, I'm sorry. I should have told you. I just thought you'd get upset. That you wouldn't understand . . . it was no big deal."

"Tate, I trust you. But we both need to learn to trust each other. Deal?"

Nigel was even sexier when he talked like that. I examined his face. His hair was held back with gel. Having his hair off his face showed those striking blue eyes even more. He was gorgeous.

"Deal," I said with excitement. I loved him so much. I should give him more credit. He had never been aggressive toward me—he'd only showed me his love, support, and care. Maybe my not telling him about going to the mall with Zach gave him the impression I didn't respect him or I was hiding something?

Nigel stepped away from the table and quickly returned with a small box wrapped in red with white hearts and a pretty bow on top. "That's for you after we eat."

I wondered if it came from Famous-Barr. I went over to my purse and took his gift out, placed it next to mine on the table, and took my seat. "That's for you after we eat."

"It's a Kinks CD."

"What?" How did he know?

Nigel laughed. "Nothing, let's eat."

I couldn't believe it. My surprise was lost.

"So Lester got the flights for Bren and me. We leave the morning of April seventh—it's a Saturday. I won't get back until the following Saturday. I've talked to

Jessie and Tommy, and they agree to keep you company while I'm gone."

"Company? Uh, I don't need a babysitter, but thanks for thinking of me." Not sure how I felt about the chaperones. It could be from a controlling standpoint, or a sincere I-don't-want-you-lonely-while-I'm-gone standpoint.

"Tatum, that's a whole week I won't be here. Let me do this one thing."

I put my fork down. "Okay, then tell me exactly why you're doing this. Because in case you haven't noticed, I have friends. And be honest, please."

Nigel copied me and put his fork down too. "Honestly?"

I nodded.

"Don't get mad."

I could feel my shoulders tense.

"Zach."

"Again, didn't we just go over this?" My hand came down on the table. "Just stop. I've told you over and over, when are you going to believe me? He is a friend, That's it."

"You showing up at the mall without telling me speaks volumes. Fine, something else bothers me. Why does he just show up at your house after school?"

"Tomorrow morning I'll tell him he isn't welcome anymore."

"No. That's not what I'm saying."

"Then say it, Nigel. Because something deeper is going on."

"Fine. I don't care if he stops by every day. If that's what you want."

He was tricky. *If that's what you want* . . . code for

"test." *Don't screw this up, because the net is ready.* I'd watched my mom and dad fight.

"I'm glad you don't care, because a jealous boyfriend is something I had to deal with before, and it didn't end well. What I do want is for the two of us not to fight over Zach, because he's only a friend of mine."

His chin lowered, and his eyes intensified. "I'm not jealous of him, not unless he touches you and you like it." With his palms down on the table, on each side of his plate, he didn't take his eyes off me. "I. Don't. Trust. Him. He's still in love with you."

Straight face. Straight face. He's good. I took a deep breath. *I understand.* "You said you trusted me."

A wickedly beautiful grin spread across his kissable mouth. "You are so good. I told you I do." Nigel walked over to my chair and pulled me up into his arms. "I love you. And I do trust you."

He brought his lips down to mine and held the side of my head. His tender embrace over my ears sent a zing down my spine. I couldn't help but react to the energy between our lips. The top of my dress became tight.

He backed away and shoved the plates away from us. Without another second wasted, he pushed my back against their Spanish table and stood in between my knees.

"M'lady, I trust you more than anybody." Nigel took his lips down my cheek, kissing down my neck, to my chest. He stopped there and stared up into my eyes. "I want you."

Nigel's beautiful eyes that spoke safety and love dug into my soul. I couldn't think. My mind went blank.

Was he asking for what I thought he was asking for? I sat up, and he put his hands behind my back for support, waiting for my answer.

"I'm not ready for sex."

"Anything but?"

I had never been in a situation like that before. Was it normal for your boyfriend to ask what he could do to you? I loved him even more with the respect he'd shown me. "No intercourse, Nige. Sorry. Just not ready for that."

"That is your call. I'll love you no matter what."

Nigel accepted my restrictions, and if there was one thing I learned, it was that guitar players knew how to use their hands.

I kept the prior evening's events to myself. The last thing I wanted to do was get Zach roiled up. So come lunch, I made a point of keeping the focus on Di and her evening with Tommy.

"So, share with us. Where did Tommy take you?"

"This cute little restaurant in the Central West End. You and Nigel would like it, Tate."

Nope. No, we wouldn't. Stop talking about me and Nigel.

Zach flipped me a sideways glare. His jealousy was getting worse too. "Not sure we would. So, did you do anything after dinner? A movie?"

Di wiggled in her seat, moving her salad around. "Nope. Nothing."

"Is that what we're calling it now?" I snickered.

Andi laughed with me, choking on some of her pizza. "Ha . . . yeah, sure. *Nothing!*" Andi's voice went higher.

Not sure why, but it was obvious if you looked at the guys they didn't like our conversation much. "Andi? What did you guys do?"

She glanced at Matt. He said nothing but watched her with his arm resting on the back of her chair. "We went to Bertano's with his parents for dinner and then we did *nothing* back at his house."

We couldn't hold it. Simultaneously, us three girls busted into laughter fits.

"Tate, what did you do?" Zach asked.

I turned to him and my laughter evaporated. "Oh, um, noth . . . dinner at his house."

Zach's glare pierced a hole through my eyes. "Were you going to say, *nothing*?"

"No." The truth was, we hadn't done much of anything. Of course, that was exactly the way I preferred my time with Nigel. He didn't need to take me shopping or out to the movies or anywhere to show me how much he loved me and how good we were together. That was the one thing I loved about him. We could do *nothing* for real, just sit by a fireplace and be happy.

Andi and Di sobered next.

Zach collected his lunch tray and walked away without another word. The three of us girls all looked at each other. But Matt shook his head. "Andi, don't wait for me. Go to class."

Matt walked away, clearly going after Zach.

"Okay, did I miss something?" I asked them.

Di played with her salad. "Nope. In the dark with the rest of us. Andi?" Di popped her stare towards Andi.

Andi's eyes lowered. "Oh, all right. Tate, he loves

you. There. Now you know the truth. He's jealous of Nigel."

I threw a roll at her. Di followed my lead and did the same. What could I do about two guys who were both jealous of the other? One I was dating, and the other I had dated.

"Smartass," I said to Andi.

We laughed about it, but the truth was it did hurt me to see Zach so miserable. But he was engaged, that was his problem, but I wasn't clueless as to how he felt. I was sure hearing everyone having dates for Valentine's Day didn't make the strongest person immune to sappy feelings.

"I'm going to go find him. I want to make sure he's okay and not going to drink." I collected my things.

"Uh-huh, sure. Just keep telling yourself that, sweetie. Do you want me to come with you?"

"No, Di. And for your info . . . I mean what I say, because it's how I feel." I turned and left the cafeteria to find Zach. I heard Matt's voice when I turned the corner, near the front lobby of the school. It was almost always empty there so it made sense they went there.

"What do you want Tate to do? Break up with the Brit the moment the princess leaves? Come on . . . get real."

I stopped and put my back to the wall to listen in.

"I know. But if she only understood my plan."

"Your plan isn't going to happen today anyway. Let her have fun . . . I mean, let her be happy for now. Because when the shit hits the ceiling with Princess . . . Tate won't be too happy. How is it going with Bonita?"

"As of last night, fine. Bonita is good. She's in. She told Mariacella since they're going to be family soon, they should act like it. Did you know about my mom going to her over the holidays?"

"Who? Catalina going to Bonita? No."

"Huh. Okay. Forget I said anything."

I didn't want to get caught listening in since they had to walk toward me for our lockers. I took off in a sprint to my locker and found Andi and Di.

"Did you find him, Tate?" Andi asked.

"Uh, yeah. Andi, keep your ear open about the princess and a plan, will ya?"

"Sure." She glanced at Di.

"Tate, what happened?" Di asked.

"They'll be coming any second, but Zach has a plan for Princess, and I gotta find out who Bonita is."

"Bonita is Tyler's girl," Andi said.

Di and I both looked at her. "Okay, well, she's in on Zach's plan," I said.

Andi closed her locker and checked the hall for the guys. "Trust Bonita. From the way Matt talks, she's next in line, after Tyler's parents."

"I don't care who's next, I'm not comfortable with Zach getting more and more into that family business. But see, this is why we will never work. He is what he is." I got in my locker and didn't say another word about my ex. Maybe overhearing Zach and Matt wasn't the best, but then again, it's constant validation I'm where I should be.

CHAPTER 12

Tatum

Friday, April 6ᵗʰ, 1990

KNOWING THIS WAS OUR LAST night together before Nigel left for England was a barbed-wire pill to swallow. Going from being together almost every day after school and on the weekends down to nothing, not even a phone call, was unthinkable.

Nigel had a hard time keeping his hand off my knee while he drove away from my house.

"So, what's for dinner, Nige?"

"Sorry, nothing special. How about the grill next to Sears at the mall? Then I thought we could watch a movie at my dad's house."

"Sounds good to me." In the past month, Nigel and I had spent a lot of time over there, with friends and alone. Every time we pushed the intimacy envelope even further, but he never pushed me all the way. He wasn't like that.

Nigel kept glancing over at me with his beautiful mouth in a relaxed grin, enticing me to kiss his lips.

When we arrived at the restaurant, the hostess sat us

in a cozy corner for two. Over the top of my menu, I could feel him staring at me. I glanced up, and he had a big smile on his face. "Nige, something going on?"

"Nothing. Just taking in every minute I have with you. I'm going to mi—"

"Stop. We're not talking about that, you'll make me cry."

He put his menu down and took my hand. "It's going to be an awful week."

The waitress showed up, and we placed our order. The second she put her back to us, Nigel leaned toward the table. "I'll call you at least once. I'm sure Lester won't mind."

"Don't worry about it, it's going to be expensive. And then if you do call, it'll probably just make it worse for me."

"Really?"

"Yeah, I'd rather just put the time in and not have you close, but not close enough."

"Guess that makes sense." Nigel relaxed.

"So tell me what you have planned. What are your stopping points?"

"Obviously, Dad's flat in Surrey. My aunt died a couple of years ago, so no more family there. But we still have friends. And visit my dad's grave."

Nigel talked for a solid ten minutes about his agenda. I was excited for him. I would give anything to go to England. Grandma and I had talked about going before she died, but we never made the trip before the cancer took her life.

While he excitedly talked about his trip, I couldn't take my eyes off his face. The skin around his mouth moving in a seductive way with the sexiest British accent made me sit a little taller. I took every word that came out of that gorgeous mouth and stapled it to my memory. I would miss him so much during his trip.

He laughed about Bren's drunkenness during a previous trip back home. His eyes brightened and sparkled. His sister was a pain in the ass to him, but he loved her. I admired that about them. I could only hope Toni would still like me when she became a teen.

The delivery of food awoke my senses and brought me back to the dinner table.

Nigel sat there leaning forward. "Tate, you okay?"

I looked up to meet his stare and discovered his caring eyes worrying about me. I could feel my mouth spread into a gentle smile. He mimicked me.

Nigel was so gorgeous. He was it for me—the one who could love me more than anything, admire me, respect me, care for me and want me.

Something clicked in my head, like a donkey had sucker-punched me in the gut. "Let's leave . . . now. I want you to take me somewhere we can be alone. No more waiting. This is what I want. Now!"

Nigel dropped his fork along with his mouth.

The waitress showed up as if she knew.

"Miss, could we get this boxed real fast? And the check, please," Nigel asked her.

She ran off.

Nigel glanced around the restaurant for a moment before focusing on me. "M'lady, are you sure? Not nice to tease me like this."

"I'm not. I swear. We've been serious for over three months now, it's time."

Within two minutes, we paid cash and ran out with our to-go boxes.

"I don't know, Tate. Are you sure? You're not rushing because I'm leaving tomorrow?"

"I'm not rushing. It just hit me when you were talking. I am madly in love with you, Nigel. If you asked me to spend the rest of my life with you, I'd say, yes! I love you."

The big Mercedes engine roared. It didn't take long before Nigel pulled into the driveway of his dad's house.

"Here, Nige? Are you sure?"

"Never more sure of anything. Remember, it's my house."

Nigel got out of the car, walked me inside through the garage, and locked the door behind him. He stopped in the kitchen, spun around to my face, and took my hands. "Stay here. I won't be but a minute." He kissed my lips and ran off.

"Not in the master. That's your parents," I yelled.

I heard him upstairs in the spare room. We had spent most of our alone time in the master, not much upstairs.

What could he be doing up there? Something nice for us? Knowing him, yes. He's so considerate. I pulled open the fridge and there sat a lonely bottle of champagne. Perfect. I checked the drawers for candles and a match. After I collected the goodies I'd accumulated in the kitchen, I set them up in the dining room. The table was set. Candles, champagne, dinner on expensive china . . . the only thing missing was a lit fireplace.

Otis Redding began singing "These Arms of Mine" over the speakers in the house. I heard Nigel coming downstairs, yelling, "Okay, m'lady. I'm back."

I stood at attention and waited for him to see the surprise I had for him.

Nigel stepped around the dining room corner. "Hey there, you—" His gorgeous blue eyes popped wide open. "Oi, m'lady."

"Well, I just wanted to do something nice for you. You always make everything so perfect, why can't I?"

Nigel wrapped his beefy arms around me and took my mouth like it was his lifeline. He lifted my ass, giving me the boost so I could wrap my legs around him. Nigel walked me up the steps, not missing a beat. Once we got to the top step, the fragrance of jasmine and vanilla warmed my senses.

Nigel placed me on the bed and backed away. His stare was undressing me. A few candles and a small table lamp cast the only light upstairs, just enough for us.

"Nigel, I love you with all my heart. We're perfect for each other, and I believe you agree with me. I want this to happen."

"Please tell me now before this goes further . . . are you sure? Sure? This isn't just fooling around in the tub. Or by the fireplace with a movie on."

I sat up on my elbows. "I've told you how many times—I'm sure. You're starting to make me think you don't want to."

He pulled his shirt over his head, exposing an impressive set of abs. I did my best to swallow the pine cone in my throat. *Dear Lord . . . give me the strength.*

Nigel unzipped his pants, and his jeans dropped to the floor. No, he wanted to. Then that second thought crept in my head: *Was I?*

No going back. I loved Nigel and wouldn't tell him no. Not that I couldn't say no. Either way, he would respect that. We loved each other. We'd been dating almost four months. We were committed to each other.

Fully unclothed, Nigel crawled onto the bed on his hands and knees.

He stopped over my body. "You still okay?"

I examined his mouth. "Yes." I put my hand up on his soft cheek. "We've been playing around for months, but not once have you pushed me all the way. You've been very respectful. I'm serious about my commitment to you. Hope you feel the same?"

"Exactly. This is forever with you and me. I never want to hurt you. Never."

"Do you have a condom?"

"I do," he said and then kissed the inside of my hand.

Nigel straddled me and pulled my sweater over my head. It had been a good idea to wear sexy underwear the night before he left. He stared at my pink lace bra, devouring my breasts with his eyes. He didn't waste time sliding the bra straps off my shoulders.

Nigel brought his face down to mine, his weight resting on his hands, baring his flexed biceps. "I love you so much, m'lady."

I had to take a deep breath and focus on my breathing with his soft lips trailing delicate kisses all over my body. Nigel was in my bubble of comfort, mind, body, and soul. His body was wrapped around mine. I trusted him and knew he would take care of me.

Nigel didn't leave an inch of my skin untouched.

Like never before, he had my body requesting more and more.

I wasn't technically a virgin, but I thought of this as my first time and that was just fine. If you had asked me eight months before whether I planned on waiting until my wedding night, I would have firmly answered, *yes*! It meant a lot to me to be intimate with as few people as possible. That meant a lot, and still did. That's why I've made this call. Nigel could be my husband. He was husband material. This was my decision, not his.

Nigel and I were both ready to take that final step. I gave him a tender squeeze. He made his move.

I tilted my head upward, trying to catch my breath. Nigel stopped and waited for my okay, and after the initial shock, I was okay. He was gentle. Everything I hoped he would be.

Fantasizing about how my first time would be had been a waste of time, because Nigel was better than anything I'd dreamt of. He was perfect.

Afterward, we both lay on our backs, our chests rising and falling to catch our breaths. He turned his head toward me, and I rolled my head toward him.

Nigel smiled at me. "I'll be back." He went into the restroom, and I followed a moment later.

"Shit," he mumbled.

"Nigel, what is it?"

He froze, standing near the trashcan. "Nothing."

I stepped inside the bathroom and over to the sink. I washed my hands and checked my hair. "You sure?"

"I'm sure. How are you?"

Nigel washed and then pulled me to him.

"I'm perfect."

Nigel's warm, swollen lips kissed me again. He took a breath. "Shall we eat some cold food?"

"Maybe we can nuke it for a minute?"

After eating a warmed dinner, we watched *Roman Holiday* by the fireplace.

Resting against pillows and wrapped in blankets watching the movie, I couldn't believe what we'd done. I was glad we had, no regrets. But knowing I gave Nigel my trust was remarkable to me. I had never let anyone hold that badge. Until now. Everything in my life was going exactly how I wanted.

My body was so relaxed I could have fallen asleep if it weren't for Nigel periodically nibbling on my neck. Maybe watching Audrey and Gregory running around Rome dancing and having champagne and gelato put him in the mood again.

After the movie, we put the house back the way we'd found it. The evening quickly slipped away from us.

In the car leaving his place, he didn't wear the same smile he had when he'd picked me up. He did keep his hand on my knee, though, and I kept my hand on his leg. I didn't want him to pull up in front of my house because that meant it was time to say goodbye, and I wasn't ready.

The Psychedelic Furs were singing "Heaven" and I couldn't stand to hear anything about planes and not cry. "Nige, could you turn that off?" He turned the dial and the CD went silent.

Nigel pulled up in front of my house, and the moment he shifted into park, we both leaped for each other. He felt like heaven around my body.

He held me close. "I'm going to miss you so much,

m'lady."

"I miss you already." I sniffled.

Nigel held his mouth on my neck. "Don't cry, I can't take it, it's killing me. I'll be back before you know it. I don't want to ever leave you again."

"What are we going to do when you leave for college this summer?"

He backed away and grabbed my face. "We will work something out. I can't live without you."

With the streetlight shining in the car and the dash lights, I could see well enough. I watched every breath he took. There was something relaxing about watching him breathe. Time stood still long enough for me to memorize the moment.

He wrapped his arms around me and took my lips for the last time for eight days. I gently caressed his ears with tears sprinting down my face. This week would suck.

He backed away and forced a grin. "Until next Saturday."

"Come over the moment you land?"

"Of course. I'll call you first."

I touched the side of his face and ears one last time. The sprinkler started again. I stepped out of the car. "Love you, Nigel."

"Love you more, m'lady."

I turned to wave goodbye and then walked in the side door. That would be the last time I saw him for one hundred and ninety-two hours and counting.

The room was bright when the shuffling around of my family getting out the door woke me. For a second I was disoriented and forgot I wasn't in bed with Nigel. Nigel. He was gone. I glanced at my clock on the nightstand. It read nine thirty. Nigel had left two hours ago. Knowing he was in the air put that cinderblock back on my chest. Only another one hundred seventy-something more hours before he returned. This week was going to suck.

I heard the front door shut and Dad's van start. They were heading out for their regular Saturday routine, which so happened to be their Sunday routine as well—breakfast out, then shopping. That was at least half the day I could spend crying in peace.

If there was one thing that made me happy, it was listening to the *Dirty Dancing* soundtrack. I popped the cassette in and blasted "Cry to Me." Standing before the floor mirror, I crossed my arms around my body and felt what Nigel had just eleven hours before. I could almost feel his breath tickling my skin again as he kissed my body. I was all alone in my room, and I could only imagine his scent, which drove me crazy knowing I couldn't see him for another whole week. Solomon was speaking my language; he understood. I felt like crying. Crying for another eight days, until Nigel got back.

That was, until the phone rang, interrupting my daydream.

"Hello?" It came out breathy. Suppose my dirty dancing in front of the mirror was more strenuous than I thought.

"So how are you surviving so far?" Di asked.

"Ha, I'm not. And it's only been twelve hours since he left."

"You want company?"

"Sure."

"Be there in ten."

Just enough time for me to get cleaned up. I wasn't showering, Nigel's scent was staying on me for at least another day.

Di walked in the house, "Hey, I'm here. You decent?"

"Yup, come in the bedroom."

She walked in and eyed me up and down.

"What? Why are you staring?" Did she notice a hickie I hadn't?

"Nothing, just a feeling," Di said with a smirk.

"Okay, shall we play the full-length version or cut to the chase?"

"So what did you and Mr. Sexy do last night for your last night together?"

"I'm sorry, not sure what you're implying but—"

"Tatum, go shower. I can smell it."

"What—"

"Sorry, I have a better sense of smell than you for certain things. Call it a talent. I'll always know if my man cheats. I can smell it a mile away."

"You're a freak." I didn't admit I could smell it too, but I wanted to. Made it more real. Kept it alive. Brought the memories to the forefront of my mind.

Di reached up and pulled my hands down, forcing me to sit next to her. "Sooo . . . how was it?"

I exhaled. Why fight her, she obviously knew. "Fine."

"Oh for the love of God, that man is not just fine. Now . . . how was it?"

I had to make sure she understood my facial expression.

"Oh don't huff and puff with me. Spill your guts."

She was incorrigible. I took a deep breath and exhaled, taking my time. "I'm the luckiest girl there is."

She shrieked. "*Oh my God.*"

"Gosh."

She rolled her eyes. "Gosh. Oh my gosh. I think it's cool you agreed, Tate. All I know from Tommy is how Nigel talks nonstop at school about how much he loves you. But I knew you guys hadn't. This is a big step for you."

"Do I really need to shower? I wanted to keep his scent on me for as long as possible, but not if it's that obvious."

"That's so cute it's sick. No, you should be okay. Just don't sit next to your parents."

Great. Now my conscience kicked in. The phone rang again. "Hold on." I reached for the receiver. "Hello?"

"Tate, hi," Zach said.

"Hi, Zach."

"I was wondering if you're busy. I would take you out. I'm assuming he's gone?"

"Zach." I stopped myself from huffing into the phone. Out of the corner of my eye, I could see Di shaking her head. "Hey, you know . . . I appreciate the offer, but I think I'm just going to hang out with Di today. Besides . . . you're making things complicated for me. This whole thing with you needs to stop. I'm sorry. Have a good weekend. Bye." I hated doing it, but I hung up.

"So he wanted to do something, I take it?"

I sat back down on the bed. "Yeah, he's just not

getting that I'm in love with Nigel."

"And he won't until you're cruel. Maybe not even then."

"Well, I hope he doesn't push me to that. I mean, I'm just not in love with him anymore."

"Then be ready this week. He will push you."

Gizmo barked in the backyard, and then we heard him running through the doggie door. After my parents had figured out Gizmo could open the door if he wanted to, but clawed the heck out of the door trim in the process, they decided to install his own doggie door. I didn't object.

I looked out the window after hearing a car door slam. "Damn it . . . what is wrong with him?"

"What?" Di rolled over to the window and looked out. "Zach." Di went back to her spot. "Told ya."

"Yeah, you sure did. Ugh . . . why do you have to be right?" I got up and walked out of the room.

"He will push you to be cruel."

I hated being pushed. And I hated being cruel. Why was he doing this?

I flung the door open and planted my feet. "And what did I just tell you?"

He walked past me, heading toward my bedroom. "You rambled on about something, but I didn't listen." He turned the corner. "Hey, Di."

I slammed the front door so hard the wall shook.

"Zach? You are asking for it," Di breathed.

"I can ask all I want, Tate will do what she wants anyway. So what does it matter?"

I stomped into my room and kept my distance from him. He was pushing his luck. Because I only had, and only wanted, Nigel on my mind. I missed him so much. I lifted my arm up to my nose and smelled. Nigel. I could smell him on me. He had such a nice scent of Beachwood and cedar.

Di and I didn't say anything, just glanced at everything in the room, but for Zach.

"All right, I obviously interrupted something. What's going on?" Zach huffed.

I wasn't about to tell him what had happened. It was none of his business. "Are you listening this time? I said you're making things complicated for me. And Di and I are doing girl stuff."

Di stood up and took a deep breath, then walked near me. "You might as well know . . . you'll find out soon enough. We were talking about how Tate slept with Nigel last night."

What the . . . "*Di!*" I shouted.

"Tate, he's going to find out soon enough. Just get it out and move on. Now you're not the one being cruel. I am."

"Maybe. But that was not your business to tell."

"True. But why dance?"

Di should have been happy she stepped past me, otherwise I would have been strangling her. "Seriously?"

"Is it true?" Zach stepped up to me, voice colder than the North Atlantic, and an expression darker than Chucky's.

With a calming breath, I faced him. He was fighting anger, but his eyes rolled downward.

"Does it matter?"

"In the grand scheme of things, no. But I would like to know."

"It's none of your business, Zach."

He grabbed my shoulders and squeezed. "Fine. It matters. If my family finds out and I'm still spoken for you, I will have to answer to Gramps. I need to have a plan if it comes to that."

The heck I would tell him anything because of his Gramps. How could that man still run my life?

"Tate, tell me now."

"Yes. I screwed his brains out. There. Ya happy?"

Di came from the side, and with one arm around my waist, she jerked me over to her like a ragdoll.

Zach turned, and a violent growl came from his chest as he shoved his fist through my wall. "Damn it, Tatum," he yelled and tugged at his hair. He spun around and took a few deep breaths.

Zach was not taking the news well. The big hole in my wall was a good indicator.

I took one step toward him but Di pulled me back and shook her head. Maybe he needed another minute before I said anything more. But I didn't need another fricking hole in the wall. How was I going to explain that to my parents? There were times I knew pushing Zach was safe, but this was not one of those times.

He spun around. The whites of his eyes expanded and he pointed to the floor. "This news does not leave this room."

"Zach, I understand you're upset, but—"

"You understand? That's funny." His laughter was forced. "You understand nothing. When Gramps finds out, my ass is on the next flight out. What's the purpose of being here when the girl who I insist will one day marry me is sleeping with someone else? You think Gramps will be fine with that? He's not a fool."

"I'm not making a fool out of him—"

"Oh, just me?" He laughed. But the kind of laugh you knew came before someone chopped your hand off.

"I'm not making a fool out of anyone."

"I am soo screwed." He jerked his head and stared at me. "You know you're killing me. You. Are. Killing. Me."

"I'm sorry. I just ask to keep things between the two of us strictly friends, no more going out together. Zach, hear me, I'm in love with Nigel."

He took a cleansing breath. "Okay. I get it. My problems are not yours. I'll call Matt to help me fix the wall. Sorry I flipped." Zach opened his mobile and dialed.

Zach accepted what I had asked him to, so why did I feel so bad? Or did he accept?

The happy high Nigel left me with Zach just pulled me from to chuck it on the floor, and then crush it further with his boot. And why couldn't my actions not have consequences on Zach's life? Why couldn't they just be my consequences?

CHAPTER 13

Tatum

Saturday, April 14, 1990

NIGEL WAS DUE BACK ANY minute. He must have put a postcard in the mail the moment he landed in England, because it had arrived in the day's mail. The postcard pictured Big Ben. Nigel wrote about how much he loved me and how he planned on coming to my house the second he got a car. He was scheduled to be at my front door in minutes and I couldn't wait.

Not seeing him for eight days after we'd made love for the first time hadn't been the easiest. Then reminding Zach day after day that we weren't going to the mall, or to the movies, or to dinner for the week was downright exhausting. Di had been right, and he pushed me many times.

My mom's grandfather clock struck six o'clock. Where was Nigel? He landed an hour and a half ago. My parents wouldn't be out to dinner for long.

Just then Gizmo barked once and then sat next to my leg. I ran over to the door and saw Nigel getting out of the Mercedes. He was home!

I ran outside as fast as my legs would take me. Nigel noticed, and the biggest smile graced his handsome face. A sexy five-o'clock-shadow looked awesome on him. He opened his arms, and I leaped for them.

He steadied us and met my lips with equal force. "Oh, m'lady . . . I missed you soo much."

"Nigel, I missed you more."

He continued kissing my lips. The safe, comfortable, loving potential life embraced me.

Nigel held me tight. "You ready? We'll get dinner and then go over to my house."

"Yeah. Let me put Gizmo up and lock the doors. Be right back."

Nigel drove us to my favorite café. We sat at a corner table, and I couldn't wait to hear all about his trip. "So, how was Bren? Any drunken stories this time?"

"Oh, she got smashed our first night. Lester was pissed and threatened to not take her back. The next day she paid for it, though. That was the most gruesome hangover I've ever seen. Lester thought that was punishment enough because he took me on the Parliament tour while she expelled her insides. The tour was fascinating."

"Order for Nigel," an employee called out.

Nigel came back with our food. The soup smelled great, and the salad was crisp.

In between bites he told me more about going back to their old flat. Nigel's mom wanted to sell the property, but Lester thought it was a good idea to save it in case Bren or Nigel wanted the home. They clearly had no issue with owning multiple properties. During the school year they would sublet it to students, but it sat vacant in the summer.

"I want to take you there, Tate. Maybe one day we'd even live there."

"Does it have a big soaking tub for two?"

Nigel's eyes drooped and he tucked in his lips. "There isn't one, but I'll put whatever you want in the house."

He was cuter than a baby squirrel discovering a birdfeeder with his naïve excitement.

"We'll see, maybe one day."

Nigel took a deep breath and a bite of his sandwich. If I read him correctly, because this had happened many times over the past four months, he wished I could go along with him. Whatever idea he had for the future, he wanted me to be just as excited as he was. I was getting better about dreaming. But I always felt a nagging in my gut, warning me to never get excited about dreaming of my future with a guy. Not only was my reaction annoying to Nigel, but the lack of enthusiasm was annoying to me.

"You know, I could see myself living there with you. From hearing you talk about it, I already feel as if I've been there."

Nigel sat up. "Brilliant. One day, Tate. One day."

"For sure, I'll hold you to it."

The content smile was back on Nigel's face. Was that so difficult for me to allow him some happiness? I really had to get better about that. They don't call it wishful thinking for nothing.

"Enough about my trip. I want to hear how your week went."

"Pretty uneventful. Just an occasional sleepover and mall trips. Otherwise, not much. Nothing like a trip to England."

"Did Jessie hang with you? Or Di and Tommy?"

He wanted to know if I'd seen Zach. That was exactly what he was digging for. I knew his jealousy had gotten bad before he left, but this thing with him and Zach had to stop. "To be exact, I saw Zach once. I have friends, you know. I don't want you getting jealous because I saw him."

"Me? Jealous? I didn't say anything about him."

"Uh, yeah, try to play Mr. Innocent with me . . . it won't work." We both laughed and changed the subject back to his trip.

After dinner, Nigel drove us straight to his house. Bren's car sat in the drive. Nigel pulled in behind her.

"Oh . . . we won't be alone? I mean, I knew Val and the others are coming over, but Bren too?" I asked.

"We will. Don't worry." He parked and turned to me. "I love you, Tate."

He could say those words a million times and they would never get old. He knew how to make my heart skip a beat. I ran my hand down his cheek. His short beard was surprisingly soft to the touch. "Love you too."

He gave me a tender kiss and we walked inside the house holding hands. Inside the door Bren came running over to me, took my left hand and began examining my fingers.

She looked at Nigel with disgust.

"Um, are they polished to your liking?" I asked. What was her deal?

Nigel was clearly put out by the assortment of sounds he made. "Damn it, Bren."

"What? What am I missing?"

"This," Nigel reached in his pocket and turned to me. In his hands rested a small ring type box. He opened the lid and there was the prettiest silver art deco ring with intricate scrolling around a small diamond.

"Tatum, this was my grandmom's, my dad's mom. I want you to have it as a promise ring. Don't look at me so surprised. Smile."

I pushed the shock down my throat. "Nigel. It's so beautiful. I can't possibly—"

"Yes, you can," Bren said.

I looked at them. They both had the same beautiful smile on their faces. "Really?"

"Yes, really." Nigel took the ring out of the box and shoved the container back in his pocket. He then held his hand out, waiting for mine.

I gave him my left hand. He slid the ring on my finger. It fit perfectly.

"We're not engaged, yet, but this is a start."

The diamond sparkled so beautifully. "Oh, Nigel." Another word couldn't come out of my mouth without making me cry. No one had ever done something so thoughtful for me before. I tossed my arms over his shoulders and kissed him. I wished Bren weren't standing there because Nigel deserved a better kiss than he got.

"Thank you. I don't know what to say. It's gorgeous."

Bren patted Nigel on his back and walked away. I guess she was in on the surprise and was supportive. Good.

"Say you'll always be mine."

I held my stare to him. "And you mine."

Nigel led me to the master and locked the door behind us. "If you don't mind, I'd like to get a quick shower in? It was a long flight."

"Are you wanting to shower or soak? I mean . . ."

Nigel grabbed my waist and pulled. "Oh, I'd prefer to soak with you, but I don't want to—"

"Go draw the water."

Nigel put a tender kiss on my forehead and went in the bathroom. "Lavender?" he called out.

"Yes, please."

If I had to guess, Nigel wanted to sleep together again. Not that I didn't want to, but I understood why people said, *once you start, there's no stopping.*

I joined him in the tub, facing each other, our arms resting over the edge. "The ring can get wet, Tate."

"I didn't want to get it gunky with soap. It's so clear and sparkly."

"We had the jeweler polish the ring."

"Well, still."

Nigel slid forward, pulling my body to him. "Are you going to wear the ring to school?"

"Yes. Wait . . . unless you want me to keep it home?"

"No, I want you to wear it all the time."

"Cause if the diamond fell out or something—"

"No, no, it's fine. The jeweler inspected it too. You're all good to go. Let's talk about Prom, though."

"Okay, what about it?"

"You're still going with me, right? Tickets go on sale this week."

"Of course I'm going with you. I think the beauty you gave me sealed any future dates." I flashed my empty ring finger.

"Perfect. If you want to go to your Junior Prom, I'll

go with you."

"No thanks. I'm not going. Let's just go to your Prom, since it's your last year. We can go to mine next year."

"Brilliant. I'll get tickets. Shall I take you shopping for a dress?"

"Uh, no, unless you want to. Or I can ask Di to go with me."

"Then I'll make dinner reservations, assuming Scotty and Tommy are in, then we'll be set. We'll triple date."

When we got out of the bathroom, the noise from a house full of people muddled the intercom music.

"Suppose everyone got here," Nigel said.

I looked at the digital clock on the nightstand. "Well, I guess so, considering it's going on nine thirty. We had to warm the tub three times."

Nigel raised his black eyebrows. "Can't rush a good thing."

He gave me another kiss and walked to the door. "Meet you out here when you're done?"

"Yeah, I'll be a minute. Need to dry my hair a bit. You got it all wet."

"That's not the only thing." He stepped outside and closed the door behind him. But the look on his face said he was quite proud of his joke.

After doing everything I needed to in the bathroom, I joined the party. Val and Di came running over. I flashed them my hand. They shrieked.

Di grabbed my palm and inspected the ring. "Oh my gosh . . . is that from Nigel?"

"Considering he's the one I'm dating, yes!"

"You know what I mean. That's a beautiful promise

ring. It's so exquisite, it kind of looks like an engagement ring." Her eyebrows raised into a question.

"Di, you're so right," Val grabbed my hand next. She looked up at me.

"It's a promise ring, but he did mention, we're not engaged *yet!*"

We hopped around in a celebratory victory huddle.

"Girl . . . he loves you so much. You're lucky," Val said.

"The luckiest." I grinned in agreement.

I was the luckiest girl—until that next morning at school. Zach seeing the ring that sparkled from my hand was going to be the low of my day. No matter how rough this was going to be, he needed to move on with his fiancée.

I saw Di at her locker and called her name. She spun around and then joined my side.

"He's going to freak when he notices the ring. Will you stay by me?" I asked.

"Of course. But he has to admit you and Nigel are only getting closer."

"Well, not sure how much closer we can get anymore," I snickered.

"True. Look, he's there waiting," Di nudged her head.

"Take a deep breath." The flame that had once burned in my gut for Zach now bruised my conscience. I knew this would hurt him.

I walked up to our locker and kept my hand hidden by the books in my arm.

He ignored Di and put his shoulder on the wall,

facing me. "Did the Brit make it back across the pond okay?"

I looked at him. His eyes were nothing but caring. He knew playing the caring card with me always weakened my defenses. "He did. Thank you for asking."

I arranged my locker belongings and closed up, putting my back against the door. "Di, you wanna get to class early?"

Di's eyes got as big as a cartoon character's. She nudged her head toward my hand. I glanced down and saw my ring was exposed. I slowly looked toward Zach. I would never forget his expression. He couldn't take his eyes off the ring, but his lips were tucked tight and the bottom lip quivered ever so slightly. The time was now, and my chest hurt from holding my breath.

"What is that? From Nigel?"

I slapped my right hand over the ring. "Uh, yeah."

Zach slowly shook his head. I dropped my right hand away. He lifted my left hand closer to his face and examined the ring.

Di and I stood there, not knowing what to say.

Zach rolled his eyes up at me. They were glassy. "It's beautiful. Looks perfect on your hand." He didn't take his eyes off me as he brought my hand up to his lips and gave a tender kiss. Once his skin touched the top of my hand, the old flame flashed. I wasn't in love with him, but I didn't want him hurt either.

Zach stared into my eyes for a silent moment. We both knew what he had going on in his life meant we couldn't be together. He was accepting I was moving on. Didn't change the fact that this was the sword through his heart. His eyes spoke to me like no others. He was saying good bye for a while. Then his eyes filled with pain.

He stood tall and walked away.

Di and I watched him go down the hall toward the cafeteria, the opposite direction from our first class.

"Di, I think he's gone mad. He just up and walked away." I turned toward her.

She adjusted her messenger bag over her shoulder. "Nah. He's just letting the news sink in. But let's hope he respects you and Nigel are a couple. I'm guessing he will. He won't risk losing you."

"This sucks. I can't stand to see him hurt. Why does my happiness have to equal pain for him?"

"Two words: *his family.*"

CHAPTER 14

Zach

*U*N-FUCKING-BELIEVABLE.
That asshole Brit is good.

I stopped at Tyler's locker. "I'm leaving. Need some fresh air."

Matt and Bobby whipped around.

"What happened?" Tyler asked.

I leaned in but kept my voice down. "That Brit gave her a promise ring. And I'm not talking about something from Zales. It's a beautiful clear diamond. It's totally Tatum. Ugh." It took everything I had not to pull out my hair.

"Okay, and leaving is going to help?"

"Tyler, as much as I love her, I will cut that finger off if it means getting rid of that ring. I need to stay away until I get my head straight."

Tyler bobbed his head. "All right. See ya tonight."

"Zach, have you talked to Bonita recently?" Bobby asked.

"Yeah, last night. I probably talk to her more than Tyler does." The way Tyler rolled his eyes, he knew it was true.

"Don't worry. Mariacella is going to make a mistake soon. The whore has to."

"I know, Bob. Thanks. But at this point I'm not sure it matters anymore. I'm too late."

I walked out of school without another word. That was the sad fact—I was too late. Tatum was in love with Nigel. Even if she really loved me, it didn't matter, she was in too far with the Brit. Tatum wasn't the type to just up and leave for no good reason. My chances were gone. A ring that was beautiful enough for Tatum's hand didn't mean just anything. He loved her, and maybe they should be together. Maybe she was right all along. Maybe I had it all wrong.

I went home, and when I walked in the door, Mom thought she was seeing double. "Zacharia, what happened?"

"Nigel. Nigel happened." I slammed my books down on the table. "Damn it."

"What did he do?"

The idea of losing Tate overwhelmed me. I couldn't imagine us apart. Tears filled my eyes like a baby. I swiped the back of my hand across my eyes. "He gave Tatum the perfect promise ring. But if you ask me, it looks more like an engagement ring."

Mom pulled out a chair and made me sit, she sat next to me. "You saw it this morning?"

I nodded.

"Okay, it's not the best news, but we can still work with this. Doesn't mean it's over."

I leaped out of the seat. "Wake up, Mom. It's over." I spun around to face her. "She's in love with him. There's a ring. End of story."

"Look, there's one more month of school, then you

can go back to Italy and get this wedding called off."

"What's the point? I'll never have Tate now anyway." I flopped myself back in the chair.

"Not with that attitude, you won't."

"Maybe I should just marry Mariacella. Catch her cheating on me and then get it annulled after I get her dad's vineyard."

Wait. If I wasn't in such hurry, maybe I could still get that vineyard. That Brit wouldn't last forever. Then when Tate leaves him, or he leaves her, I'd be ready to move forward. Yeah. That was still my way out of the business. Get the vineyard first. So, maybe I'd have to marry the tramp. She'd screw up soon enough.

"Mom, that's how I get the vineyard . . . we need to make sure Gramps puts in the prenup that the vineyard is mine upon marriage. I'm getting that vineyard, and then a divorce."

Mom patted my knee as she stood. "Yes, that's a perfect idea. The time for Tate will come. Focus on getting this vineyard first. I'm proud of you, son." She walked into the office.

I picked up the phone by the door and dialed Bonita. "Any news?" I asked after she answered.

"Okay, I know Catalina is good, but that's ridiculous."

"What?"

"I was just getting ready to call you. Cat must have sensed it and told you. Anyway, last night after I talked to you, Mariacella called me, and she wants to throw a big party before her fiancé gets back home. This could be it."

"Oh, you've got to be kidding me."

"No, how come you don't sound happy?"

"Nothing. I am happy. So when is this party taking place?"

"Not sure. She was throwing around dates. Maybe May nineteenth or the twenty-sixth. She didn't know. Sounded like she was trying to have it before you're out of school. Guess she wants to make sure you won't be back. I know she's been doing things, but never with me there or knowing about it. But the way she talks, she's screwing around."

"I guarantee she's screwing around. Okay, from here on out, my last day of school is June first. That way it gives me more time to let Tate know I'm leaving again. I'd definitely shoot myself in the foot if I up and left her again without warning."

"When are you out of school?"

"Didn't Tyler tell you?"

"No, we haven't talked about it."

"This is perfect. I'm not telling you. June first is all you do know."

"I see."

"I'll make sure the others know to say June first too. Then the moment you get more news on this party she wants, you call me. I don't care what time it is. Call me."

"Got it. Hope you know what you're doing, Zach. She's crazy."

"Don't get spooked now."

"I'm not. I'm just saying, she's insane."

"Exactly why I want this over with."

After we hung up, I told Mom about the information Bonita gave me. The family had an agreement we would keep Gramps out of the sabotaging plans. He wouldn't understand. To him, it was more important to establish family stability with this deal. But the rest of us just wanted another business. This was everyone's way out.

By lunchtime I felt much better. An updated plan was in motion, and Bonita had given me the best news of all. I felt so good I went back to school. When I walked in the main doors and into the cafeteria, her long blonde hair caught my attention. Just a while longer and that girl would be mine. All mine.

Tatum spotted me when I was a couple of tables away. Her back stiffened. Then her henchwoman, Di, noticed me next and whispered something into Tate's ear.

I took my usual seat next to Tatum and smiled at her. She was so cute when she was confused.

Matt nudged his head at me. "You okay?"

I nodded to him a *yes* and turned my attention to Tatum. "Hey, I know this morning was a bit awkward. Sorry. Just needed some fresh air."

Tate relaxed. "Oh, it's okay. You were fine. Glad you feel better."

I couldn't help but take a glance at that diamond. *Ugh, that stupid Brit. Temper. Control. I have to control my temper.* "I do. Thanks. And the ring is beautiful on you. I can't lose our friendship, though. And no matter how much you love him I'm here for you."

Tatum tossed her arms around my neck. "Oh, Zach. That means a lot to me. Thank you."

Over Tatum's shoulder, Di was giving me a dirty look, shaking her head and mouthing, "Ass."

I held Tatum to me, giving her henchwoman a dirty look back. Tatum felt so good in my arms. Damn, her breasts felt like heaven against me. I wanted her. The effect she had on me headed for my groin.

I pulled away before I was stuck sitting there tucked under the table for a while. "Thanks for understanding."

She patted my cheek in a friendly gesture. "What are friends for?"

There was no way in hell that girl believed we were just friends. Didn't matter—I had to accept her game for now. But in another six weeks I hoped to have this all over with and behind me.

CHAPTER 15

Tatum

Saturday, May 5th, 1990

DI, VAL, AND I BARELY fit in my bedroom. Three sexy dresses lay across my waterbed. My mom kept popping her head in, checking up on us. But I knew it was so she could admire all of the lace, fluff, satin, and beading on my bed. Once a dress junkie, always a dress junkie.

"My stupid hair is not working today. Out of all days." I grabbed the scissors from my nightstand.

Di snatched them out of my hand. "No one is cutting anything. Sit down and let me try."

"I shouldn't have shampooed. It's too soft." I sat on the frame of my waterbed.

Di stood in front of me with her chin in the palm of her hand. Val joined her side.

They made me feel like their science project. "Oh, for the love of God," I huffed.

"First, you could use a little purple eyeshadow. Then why don't you go with soft curls? Tate, your hair looks better soft and wavy, anyway," Val said.

Di twisted and rolled her lips around, thinking. "She's right about the wavy, but you know Tate likes corals, not that purple crap. Okay, sit still."

Di had my hair looking perfect long before Nigel and the guys arrived.

"Tatum, girls . . . the limo just pulled up." My mom came barging in my room. "It's time." She smiled at us. "Hurry." She shut the door behind her and yelled, "Ken, get the camera. The boys are here."

My friends knew my mom wouldn't be complimenting us on our looks for the dance. Whether that was my mom's typical protocol or not, it hurt.

"Okay, let's hit it." I sprayed a few last pumps of perfume and walked out. Di and Val followed me.

Our high heels clanked across the hardwood floor. We stepped outside. Scotty, Tommy and Nigel all whipped around and stared at us.

By the look on Nigel's face, he was pleased. Dad eyed Nigel with a direct *dare you* glare. Nigel was oblivious to my dad's threat, though.

Sorry, Dad.

The guys came hustling over to take our arms and walk us to the limo.

Nigel took mine but didn't take his eyes off me. "Blimey, Tate. You are amazingly beautiful. I'm so lucky."

I only smiled. Nigel didn't know that was what I said about him. "You look pretty dashing yourself. Love the sharp tux."

My mom lined us up around the limo for random photos until Dad said, "Cynthia, enough. I took about a hundred pictures. Let them go."

Mom agreed and let us load into the limo. Once I

took my seat, I glanced outside at her. She was waving like a lunatic. She couldn't voice her happiness, but she made it clear by her actions. Suppose that was second best.

You could hear the bass booming the moment we walked into the hotel lobby. The ballroom had to be close. Volunteers took our tickets and pointed out the ballroom and the photographer station for our Prom pictures.

Nigel slid his arm around my waist, giving a slight tug, and led me to the party. "Okay, now that I can say this without everyone listening, I can't wait to take you home. I want to discover everything you have tucked in the tightest dress I've ever seen."

"Well, believe it or not, not much. But the dress is very stretchy. Thank goodness since I ate too much. Dinner was great. The dress must be made of rubber bands because I can bend and sit without a problem."

"Tatum, I've never loved anyone more than I do you."

I moved toward him, leaving an inch from his lips. "I love you more."

He grabbed the sides of my face and kissed me.

"Save it for later." Scotty snickered when he and Val passed us.

Nigel wrapped his arm around my waist, and the six of us walked into the vibrating and sparkling ballroom. Val claimed the last empty table in the back.

I put my purse down and turned toward the dance floor. The disco ball hanging from the ceiling above the students shined all the way back to our table in the back row. Enough sequins to wrap around the world were on that dance floor.

Nigel leaned toward my ear. "Would you like to dance with me?"

I turned to his sultry eyes. "I would."

Nigel took my hand and twirled me around. Even in a tight dress, I was able to move freely. That was, until we reached the tenth song.

"Nigel, it's break time. I need to stop before I get sweaty."

We walked to the bar and he ordered two Shirley Temples.

I whispered to him, "You know for the boys it's called a Roy Rogers?"

"No kidding?" He handed me mine. "Brilliant names."

Suppose they didn't use silly names for their "virgin" cocktails over in England.

After we'd been sitting at the table for a while, the music stopped and the intercom clicked on. I sat there, observing the room. It truly was a magical atmosphere. The balloons. The lights. The formal gowns all of the girls were wearing screamed one heck of a party. Now I know why so many girls love Prom. Val's wiggling in her seat brought me back to the now. Why was she so excited?

A student in a white tux walked across the stage. "All right, folks, you know what time it is. Time to crown the Prom King and Queen and their court."

The crowd cheered. Di and I turned to each other and gestured, *gag me with a spoon*. Tommy shook his head at us and patted Di on her bare back. Her yellow alter dress draped open in the back to just above her rear.

The student announced the whole court but for the king and queen. "Prom Queen for 1990 is Porsche McKinley."

The room erupted in applause. Some hooted and hollered like she was a piece of meat. Di and I went to our go-to hand gesture—gag me with a spoon. They crowned her and handed her a bouquet of roses.

"And the Prom King for 1990 . . ." He opened the envelope and the card. "Is Nigel Begum."

The room erupted again.

"What did he just say?" I asked Di.

"He said, Nigel."

I turned to my other side, and Nigel was sitting there with a flask under the cloth. "Tate, pass this to Di, hurry."

I grabbed the flask and handed it over. "Nigel, I think they called you."

Everyone around us was looking at him and clapping.

"Val, did you know this?" Nigel grunted.

She giggled. "Yes! Go. They called you."

He put his cup down. "Damn it to hell." He gave me a quick kiss and walked onto the stage.

I wasn't sure what was happening. "How did you know, Val?"

"I'm on the committee and helped count the votes." She chuckled.

Di leaned toward my ear. "Holy crap . . . you're dating the Prom King."

Me? Nigel? I wouldn't be voted top of anything at my school. He must have a lot of friends. When Nigel walked onto the stage with his black tux and black tie, I would have sworn more girls yelled. That's when I surveyed the room again. Most girls were smiling and admiring my boyfriend.

They went right into the court's dance, which was a slow song. Students followed the court and stood around the dance floor's perimeter to watch their Prom King and Queen dance. I didn't care to see another girl, this Porsche, in Nigel's arms. She seemed a bit too content for my liking.

"I'll kick her ass after the dance," Di whispered in my ear.

Was my jealousy that obvious? "Get in line."

The song was almost over, and I noticed Nigel was motioning with his finger for me to come to him. He didn't need to do that twice. I got out of my seat and headed over to the side of the dance floor, excusing myself while I pushed through the crowd.

Nigel gave a slight bow to Porsche and dropped his arms from around her.

He stepped over to me and wrapped his arms around my body and began slow dancing with me. "I don't give a rat's ass about this, you're my queen."

Oh hell yes, he's so finding out what's tucked away in this dress. "Perfect, because you're my king."

The song ended and Nigel stopped and kissed my lips. His warm, soft touch sent that zing down my spine and then back up before tingling the tips of my toes. He slid his hand down to my ass and gave a squeeze.

He backed away with red lipstick smeared across his swollen lips. "Ready to go?"

"Yes. Is the limo out there?" I wiped what red I could off him.

"Yeah. We just have to go out and wave. He'll pull up."

The six of us left Prom and headed to Nigel's father's house. Bren had her friends over to "supervise." Sometimes I wondered just how delusional Nigel's mother was.

When we pulled up in front of Nigel's other house, by the looks of the lawn, everyone was partying pretty hard.

We stepped out of the limo and Nigel thanked the driver and tipped him. Di leaned toward me. "Uh, looks like Bren invited the neighborhood."

"Yeah, I'm sure Nigel isn't thrilled."

Bren came stumbling toward us. "Hey, little bro, how was the dance of a lifetime?"

"Jesus, Bren. You're already drunk."

"Mom always said you were the smart one." Bren swayed.

Vic ran over and grabbed her. "Sorry, Nigel. The girls were in there doing shots. Come on, Bren. Let's go lie down for a bit."

Bren sloppily waved as Vic escorted her inside the house.

Nigel turned around to me, forgetting his sister's drunkenness. "What do you want to drink?"

"Whatever. You know what I prefer."

He gave me a warm kiss before he and Tommy walked off to get drinks from inside the house. Di, Val, and I stood there taking inventory of the backyard. People I'd never seen before cluttered the lawn. Some playing games, others standing around just talking.

Val had Scotty's flask in her hand, taking gulp after gulp. "I can't believe Nigel was crowned Prom King. But then again . . . maybe I can."

Scotty elbowed her. "Val."

Di and I glanced at each other.

"Hey, there you guys are." Jessie walked up to us. He gave Di and me a quick hug. "Where's Nige and Tommy?"

"Inside, getting drinks."

"Right. Man . . . Bren and her friends are trashed. I swear they invited everyone in St. Louis. The house is crowded inside."

"Yeah, Vic took her inside to lie down," I said.

"So how was Prom?" Jessie asked.

Di laughed. "You didn't hear?"

"No. What?" Jessie looked back and forth between me and Di.

"Nigel was crowned Prom King," Val slurred.

"No shit? I bet he hated that."

Scotty nodded, but didn't say anything. I noticed Val wasn't stable on her feet and Scotty was holding her up.

"Crap. Don't look now, but Sam is walking this way with a stupid grin on her face," Jessie huffed.

"Who's Sam?" I asked.

Jessie and Scotty both stared at me, their eyes bigger than golf balls. Then they whipped their stare back to a girl stumbling in our direction.

Was everyone already drunk at the party?

"Just ignore her, Tate," Jessie mumbled.

"Hey, guys. I saw Nigel was crowned Prom King. I wanted to congratulate him." Sam said. The girl slurred so bad it was tough to understand her. "Where is he?"

I opened my mouth, but Jessie put his hand in front of me. "Around."

"Oh, come on, Jessie. Be a friend and tell me."

"Sam, go home. You're drunk," Scotty said.

Val tossed back the flask and swayed. "Yeah, go home. Nigel's busy tonight."

Scotty put his hand over Val's mouth and pulled her away.

Di and I gave each other warning looks. Time to step in. "Hi, Sam. I'm Tatum. Are you okay?"

Jessie shook his head and backed up.

Di stood next to me. "I'm Di. Tommy's girlfriend. So tell us, what connection do you have to Nigel?"

She took a drink from her red plastic cup. "Besides school, we met at a party one night."

Jessie stepped around Di and me and grabbed Sam. "Okay, time to call you a ride."

"Wait. Take your hands off her," I said.

He looked at me with the eyes of someone who'd failed a math class. "Tatum, you don't want to do this."

Jessie's reaction told me otherwise. "So Sam, what happened at this party? Is that how you know him? I won't judge you. You know . . . between us girls."

"Oh he said he'd take me home, but we ended up talking. And then went into a bedroom. One thing led to another."

"Okay, that's enough." Jessie grabbed Sam's shoulders.

"Jessie, don't make me kick you in the balls. Let her go. Now."

Sam's balance was worse than a toddler's.

"Like how? What led to one thing or another? I mean . . . did you?" I said, with my heart rate faster than the norm. If I didn't come off threatening, she would "trust" me. She was drunk with truth serum.

"Tate." Jessie shook his head and stormed off toward the house.

Di got closer to Sam. "It's just us, do tell. We think he's so hot. We won't say anything." Her voice was wicked.

"I'll never forget . . . Nigel and me, we talked it seemed like forever. He's the only guy I've been with who talked beforehand. We started making out and then doing it. But he stopped. I don't know why he stopped, but he did."

"When was this party, Sam? Do you remember?" Di asked.

I was glad Di said something, because my heart leaped up inside my throat from hearing my boyfriend had screwed this girl.

"Right before Christmas."

"This past Christmas, Sam?" I asked. Begging for anything besides *yes*.

Sam glanced up to the sky, but her eyes narrowed. "Yup. The Friday before Christmas. Yup." She tried to grin, but it looked more like Jack Nicholson playing the Joker in *Batman*.

In my head, I was doing the timeline as quick as I could because my heart was going to explode. Or maybe it was my gut pushing up to my chest. I felt like throwing up. *Christmas Eve was on a Sunday. That party she's talking about must have been the Friday before. Two days before Nigel asked me to go steady with him.*

"Anyway, he hurt my feelings, but I forgive—"

"Tatum?" I looked up towards the house where Nigel's voice came from. He was hustling out of the house with drinks in his hands, Tommy and Jessie in tow.

"There he is, Sam. Go congratulate him." Di turned Sam around to face him.

Nigel stopped dead in his tracks.

My chest rose, and my breath caught. He always said I should be honest with him. Be truthful with him. Love him. I did, and the hypocrite was a player.

After everything we've been through, he lied to me. He was with another girl while we were dating? We began seeing each other after Thanksgiving. Oh my God. That whole time . . . Bile shot up my throat.

His gorgeous eyes angled downward, worry written across his face.

He was no different from the next dickhead cheater.

I hiked up my dress and took off toward the street.

Di followed me. "You were seeing him then. Oh my God, Tate. Guess I'm getting the car again . . . I don't have a car here. Crap."

"No, stay here, Di." I slipped off my shoes and ran ahead of her and down the street as Nigel called after me to wait.

No matter how fast I ran, I could hear him catching up. He was faster. Stupid dress. I tried harder, not wanting to be caught.

"No, Tatum. Don't. Damn it, Tatum. Stop. Let me talk to you. Please?"

If I spoke, more energy would be wasted. I turned the dark corner and couldn't see ahead of me. I had to slow. My feet were bare and felt like they were bleeding.

I heard him breathing right before he grabbed my shoulder and pulled. "I said, wait." He spun me around.

"After everything, you lied to me, Nigel. You got me to sleep with you. Just like the next blonde."

"Stop it. I want to explain. Please?"

"Sam already did." Tears filled my eyes, and when I blinked, they came gushing down my cheeks. "It must be your trademark to talk to a girl before you sleep with them." I felt cheaper than a Cracker Jack toy.

"That isn't true. Yes. I talked to her that night. I wanted to get her to sleep it off at that house, but she wouldn't shut up and sleep. We did, but I stopped . . . feeling disgusted with myself. I had no interest in that girl, but no excuse, the liquor made it easy. I'm so sorry."

Sorry was cheap after the fact. The anger volcano erupted. I smacked Nigel. "Never talk to me again. Don't even think about calling me—coming by my house after school—nothing."

Nigel grabbed my shoulders. "You listen to me. I'm in love with you. She meant nothing." The moment those words came out of his mouth, I saw the regret creep over his face. "I didn't mean it like that."

"That's what they all say. You're no different. Let me go. Right now."

Nigel released his grip. "Tatum?"

"I am leaving." The mothership exploded from combustion. "You lied to me." The ugly cry erupted. "What have you always asked of me? To be honest with you. I have. Why didn't you tell me about her when you told me about the other three? How many girls have you already slept with?"

"Because would you have listened to me any further if you knew I slept with someone I didn't care about? What kind of guy does that make me? Whether it's fair judgment or not."

"You are what you are, Nigel. Did you think this would never get out?"

Nigel ran his hand through his hair. "No. I didn't think that through. It's my business and my shame, and I wanted it kept that way."

"Then maybe you should have thought about who you were putting your dick into first." I turned and headed back to his house.

"Where are you going?"

"I'm going to hitch a ride with someone. I'm leaving." I looked him straight in the eyes. "It's over between us."

Nigel grabbed my arm. "The hell it is. We're perfect for each other, and you know it. I love you, Tatum."

"I refuse to be with someone who doesn't practice what they preach. Now take your hand off me, right now. You're hurting me." He let me go.

The ring Nigel gave me snagged on my dress. The one thing I looked at every day to remind me of Nigel's love. I pulled the ring off my finger and walked back to him. Nigel noticed, and tears glistened in his eyes.

I grabbed his hand and slapped the ring in his palm. "It's not right for me to keep this." I turned and walked toward his house.

"Damn it, Tatum. You're not doing this to us. I won't let you."

"No one tells me what to do." I kept walking back

to his house.

When I turned the corner, I could see Di, Tommy, and Jessie standing in the front lawn, watching us.

Di came running over. Her eyes scanned my face from top to bottom. Her nostrils flared with a deep breath in and her eyes widened. She knew shit had hit the ceiling. "Tate?"

"Sorry, but I need to leave."

Nigel huffed and puffed, cussing under his breath.

Di took my hand, and I could feel what she was feeling in her grip. Everything in the perfect girlfriend displayed on her face. We both held our breath. I couldn't take the pressure of being tough anymore—I dropped my head on her shoulder and cried. I didn't care who saw. Di held me close, squeezing.

I'd fallen for Nigel. I'd fallen for the safety net and given him what I still considered my virginity. Nigel had it, and it meant nothing to him. I was just another girl he could screw. Why did I think he would be different—a guy built like him who's, caring, smart and with an accent any girl would want to listen to the rest of her life? None of it mattered to him. I was just another cheap fish in the pond.

I cried so hard I could feel the hiccups rolling to my chest.

"Shh, Tate. It's okay. Calm down," Di whispered.

"Damn it, Tatum. Let me take you inside to talk. Or if you insist on leaving, let me take you home," Nigel grunted.

I released my hold from Di and spun around. "No. You are not allowed to tell me any more lies. I won't fall for them again."

Jessie paced. "Nigel. Why didn't you tell her? We

all knew."

"Jess, don't," Tommy said.

"Shut up," Nigel yelled at Jessie.

Jessie took off toward the house.

Nigel raked a hand through his hair and yanked on the ends. "This can't be happening!"

It was one pill to swallow if Nigel and I were at each other's throats, but one too many if he was fighting with his friends.

"Di, why don't you take my car and drive Tate home. We'll worry about cars later," Tommy offered.

"I want Tatum to stay with me. We need to work this out."

"Nigel, dude . . . I get it. But you need to let things cool tonight. You're both too upset to be rational. You're yelling at everyone."

Nigel grabbed my waist before I could react and squeezed me to him. "You're not leaving me now. Not tonight. We can work this out. I know we can. I want to, Tatum. I love you. I love you more than anything."

I hated feeling good in his arms. It would have been all too easy to let him carry me upstairs and make me forget all about that Sam girl. All too easy. But it wouldn't change the fact that Nigel had cheated on me. I'd asked him how many girls he slept with, and he always said just his three past girlfriends. The first time I'd asked that question was just over a week after he screwed Sam. He didn't forget. He lied.

I put my hands on his chest and shoved. "I said no. It's over. I will not allow you to cheat on me again."

"Di, here's my keys. Take her home." Tommy handed Di the car keys and she grabbed my hand, pulling me toward his car.

I could hear Nigel yell, "Who invited Sam? I said I never wanted to see that girl again."

Di drove us away from Nigel's after-Prom party. What started out as the perfect evening couldn't have ended worse. And for some reason, my gut twisted and knotted with the feeling that it was the last time I would drive away from Nigel's house.

A half an hour later, Di and I shed our beautiful dresses and crawled in my bed. I rolled toward her and rested my head on her shoulder.

"Not once did he mention he was seeing some-one else while we were dating. Not once. Di . . . we were dating when he screwed her. Who else was he 'dating'? He could have screwed them too and been fine not telling me. And after everything . . . the jeal-ousy over Zach . . . the constant reminding me to be honest and open with him . . . this is what I find out. In front of a crowd. How embarrassing. He told me a little about his other three girlfriends before me. Nothing about who else he was seeing while with me. I thought I was the only one."

"Well, suppose that's why he kept telling you to be honest with him. He had a guilty conscience about keeping Sam from you."

I turned my head to her. "Do you think there were others? Really. What about that Porsche girl? They looked pretty cozy on the dance floor." I could feel my heart pounding, waiting for her answer.

She took a deep breath, put her arms around me and squeezed. I could feel my head wedged under her chin. "I have no clue. Tommy never told me about any of this either."

"They all kept this quiet. Even Val. Why didn't she tell me Nigel had other girls he was dating? Just let me know then. Di, think of it . . . he put his dick in another girl when we had been seeing each other for a month, and just two days before he asked me to go steady. Who does that? I had sex with him. *A lot* in the past month. That's a big deal to me. I'm so pissed."

"I know. I know. Did you guys always use a condom?"

"Yes, thank goodness." I didn't think of that before, but I was glad we'd protected each other. Who was I kidding . . . we protected *me*. He could have some funky STD. "He's planned everything for our future, Di. All for what? Is he controlling and I didn't see it?"

"No, he's protective, but not controlling. I just think he's kept some major skeletons from you."

"Other skeletons than this?"

"Honestly?"

I nodded.

"Tate, he was voted Prom King tonight. You find out he's not been honest with you about who else he was seeing while he was seeing you. He screwed a girl two days before he asked you to go steady. I think he's slept around a lot, and between his guilty conscience and getting around, he was paranoid with you. He knew you didn't sleep around and you would have judged him if you knew he did. That's just what I think. The good part is he wanted to impress you."

I lay there thinking, Di could be right. This whole time, his begging me to be honest and let him know if I preferred to be with Zach was because he feared I'd screw Zach while I was dating him. Maybe he cheated on me after he slept with Sam? Or maybe he screwed around on those other girlfriends? And he feared his darker side would be let out of the bag. He'd lied this whole time.

I wasn't sure what would happen next, but I did know Nigel messed around, a lot.

CHAPTER 16

Zach

I GLANCED AT THE CLOCK ON my dresser and it said eleven thirty. Tate had to be up and moving around. I wanted to see how Prom had gone. Of course, that meant another headache, I was sure.

I picked up the phone and dialed her.

"Hello?" Tate sounded different, not tired, though.

"Did you stay up all night?" I asked her.

"What's up, Zach?"

"Oh man . . . I've known you too long . . . what happened? Better yet, I'm coming over. Sorry, you can lecture me when I get there." I hung up.

I knew that girl better than her own mother did. She was upset and had been crying, but showing face. Something had happened. I grabbed my car keys and yelled out to my mom. "Going to Tate's, be back later."

I watched for cops, trying my best to get there. When I pulled up, her parents' van was gone. She was alone.

I hustled up to the front door and went inside.

"I'm here. Close the door behind you," Tate called

out.

I turned the corner and she was lying on her bed, still in her nightshirt and boxers. Her eyes were swollen and red. She turned away from me. That idiot did something to hurt her.

"What did he do to you? Tell me. Now."

"The short answer is, he lied and . . . cheated."

I sat down next to her, on the edge of her bed. "Cheated? What?" It came out rushed. *Temper. Can't lose my temper.*

She hiccupped a whimper. "He screwed some girl while we were dating, and then two days after they screwed, he asked me to go steady with him."

"Have you cried all night?" I swiped at the couple of tears sliding down her face.

"How long is all night?"

I grabbed under her arms and pulled her up to my chest. "Tate. Don't cry. Please . . . stop crying." If she didn't, I would be making a visit to Nigel's house. "This came out last night? At Prom?"

"Yeah, I found out from the girl he screwed. She showed up at his after party. Oh . . . and Nigel was crowned Prom King."

I backed her up and looked at her face.

She grinned. "Don't look at me like that. Yes. He was crowned."

"No shit?"

"No shit."

I couldn't help but laugh. That was the funniest thing I'd heard in a long time. I would never be voted top of anything at school.

"Come on, I feel crappy enough as it is. Stop laughing, Zach." She chuckled.

Good, she smiled. Because it was getting hard not to take off to beat the hell out that Brit when she was crying.

I wanted her in my arms. That was the only way I felt better. I slipped off my shoes and crawled in bed with her. "I don't mean to make you feel worse. Do you want to talk about it?"

"Nothing can change what happened."

"True, but how did you leave things with the old boy?"

Smile gone. She glared at me. "Stop with the piss-poor British accent. I broke up with him. I told him it was over between us."

"Did you really?"

"Yes." She didn't take her stare off me.

Tears welled up in Tate's eyes. She was going to cry again. She rolled on her side, away from me, and let it out. Curling into a fetal position.

Maybe if I let her go for a while, she'd get it all out. Maybe?

I rolled her to face me. "Tatum, I'm sorry. I know this isn't what you wanted. I wish there was something I could do. I know you won't believe me, but I can't stand to see you cry. It hurts."

Her beautiful blonde hair cascaded across her face. I swiped her bangs from her eyes. "Love? Do you want me to go talk to him?" *Please say yes.*

"Why? I don't want him. I'm the one rejecting him, not the other way around."

"Okay, do you want me to go talk to him . . . about . . .?"

"Zach." She put her hand on the side of my cheek and held me there. "Listen to me. I broke up with him. I said it was over. End of story."

Tatum's words went straight to my groin, again. She had no clue I thought we were "end of story" a month ago and look at us now. I put my hand over hers, saying, "If that's what you say, then I'm sorry."

The two of us stayed in that position for at least ten minutes. She was so beautiful. Her lips parted. They begged to be kissed.

I slid my hand off hers and continued down her neck until I reached the back of her head, and pulled. Once our lips touched, my jeans got tight in the groin. We were meant to be together. She had to know this. She had to feel the same.

Tate scooted closer to me.

I didn't let go of her lips. I wanted deeper in her mouth. With one swift move, I grabbed underneath her perfect ass and rolled us, putting her on top. Tate sat up in a straddling position and looked down at me.

We stared at each other for a moment. I had to slow my breathing.

"Tate, I love you. Always have. Always will."

She stared at me. Not a word, just stared. If I knew her, she was talking to herself. She was confused. But then she looked content.

Tate grabbed the bottom of her nightshirt and pulled it up and over her head. Her bare breasts were staring back at me. I really needed extra room in my jeans.

"Tate?"

"Maybe I should have been thinking with my heart all along."

"What does that mean?"

Tate shook her head. "Nothing." She grabbed my shirt and pulled it off me.

Tatum was talking, but I couldn't ignore those luscious breasts bouncing in front of my face. I took a breath, but I couldn't breathe. I grabbed her breasts and squeezed. Heaven in my hands.

"Make love to me, Zach?"

That caught my attention. "Huh?" One stupid thought crossed my mind: *This was not the time.* She was in pain. I couldn't touch her. Damn it if my conscience wasn't the only thing growing. I dropped my hands. *The one time she wants to and I won't.*

"Tate, not like this. I won't be used as the rebound. We're more than that to each other."

She grabbed the covers and pulled them across her breasts. She crawled off me. "I'm so sorry. I didn't mean to—"

"No, Tate. Wait. I'm just saying—"

"I get it. I've just embarrassed myself."

I grabbed her shoulder and stopped her from moving away from me. "Stop it." I squared her off to me. "I love you so much, I'm willing to start a Mob war in Italy between families. Hon, you have no clue how much I love you. How much I want to spend the night with you. To lie in the same bed as you and have your face be the first thing I see in the morning. So calm down. The time will come for this to happen. Trust me, I'll make sure of it." I ran the back of my hand down her cheek.

Damn . . . I wanted her so bad.

We heard a car door slam, and a second later the doorbell buzzed. I pulled the shade back. "It's Nigel."

Tate stood there not speaking. I wasn't sure she was

even breathing. "Nigel is going to kill me," she mumbled.

"Tatum, please open up," Nigel called from outside.

She tossed her nightshirt over her head and ran for the door. I grabbed my Zeppelin shirt off the bed and ran after her. I jotted ahead and grabbed the door handle. I wanted to rearrange the Brit's pretty face for cheating on her.

Tate stopped me. "No, I want to do this."

I let go of the doorknob. "You're right. I'll be right here."

Tate unlocked the door and slowly opened. "Nigel, I will let you in if you remain calm."

Once the door was opened enough, Nigel stormed inside and passed Tate, and before I knew it, the Brit clocked me square in the jaw.

"You piece of shit. I trusted you with her," Nigel yelled.

I swayed but caught my balance and adjusted my jaw.

Tate jumped in front of me. "How dare you come in my house slugging anyone? You said you wanted to talk, not fight."

My tough girl. She was protecting me. She was so cute. Nigel was trying to intimidate me with dirty looks. Tate turned around to me.

"Damn it, Zach. Stop laughing." She backhanded my chest.

"What?" I wasn't laughing, just amused.

Tate dropped her head and gave it a one-two shake. "Nigel, we need to talk."

"Tell me now, did you just screw him?"

"How dare you speak to me like that? I'm not

one of your whores. I changed my mind, we're not talking. Get out of my house."

This Brit had balls. "Nigel, you say one more word to her like that and I'm going to make sure you find the door."

"What are those?"

Tate and I glanced around, not knowing what Nigel was talking about.

Nigel pointed to my arms. "The tattoos. Is that your name, Tate?"

"Um—"

My pride and joy . . . about time I could show them off. "Yeah. I got these babies back in Italy." I held my forearms together.

"You know what, Tate . . . figures he's here. I knew he would take the slightest opening. Did you break up with me because of my past, or yours? You're obviously not that heartbroken since you've already screwed him." Nigel stood before her, holding her shoulders. "We can't go back now. Sorry."

Nigel pulled Tate to his lips and kissed her, hard.

Temper. Watch my temper. This is Tate's call. She wants to handle him, I'll respect that.

He dropped his grip and turned away.

"Wait, Nigel." Tate sprang forward to grab his arm.

Nigel headed for the front door. He glanced back at her but kept going.

"But we didn't . . ." Tate turned to me.

She wasn't breathing. "Tatum, breathe. It'll be okay."

I pulled her into my chest and kissed the top of her head. She smelled like lavender.

"Well, there goes that chance," she whimpered.

I held her back and looked her in the eyes. "He

also cheated on you. When you ask a girl to go steady, you're typically not screwing another girl two days before."

"But he thinks we had sex, and we didn't."

"But we could have. Let him chew on that thought for a while. Because I guarantee you he's heading to someone else's house tonight. He'll want revenge."

"Zach, you should go."

"What? Why?"

"You." She poked her finger into my chest with each word. "Are. Still. Engaged." She stepped around me and stomped into her bedroom.

I ran after her. This girl was getting my blood pressure up, and all because she felt out of control. I knew that's what she was pissed about. She was worse than a Bertano. "Hold up. I know I am. But you agreed to wait for me. Tate . . . what we have is real."

Tate spun around. "Real? What's real is Mariacella. Your wedding this summer. Those things are real, and they change the game. I don't know what I was thinking."

She spun back around and began making her bed. "I feel dirty. What am I doing? You have a fiancée. I feel like a tramp. Because I was just exposing myself to you and if Nigel did more than kiss me just now I would have let him. It's best if you go. I need to get my life in order."

"I know you're upset—"

She spun on her heels. "Upset? You know what? You know why I wanted to sleep with you?"

Those words made my heart stop. *Tatum, please don't be cruel.*

"I was going to sleep with you because I'm tired of

being what everyone thinks I am—a good girl. Do you know what it's like to continuously do things just for the sake of being what others want you to be? You have no clue what it's like trying to keep my parents off my back on a daily basis. I'm tired. It's time to focus on what I want for a change, so I wanted to sleep with you to feel better for the moment. That's all. *Upset* doesn't begin to explain my feelings." She resumed making the bed.

I was sick of her saying things she would never say to me under regular circumstances, all to chase me off. I was tired of her trying to hurt me. Tired of the sleepless nights wondering how I could have done things differently.

"You have no clue what you're talking about. You think you're the only one who has no control over their life? You're more delusional than they are. So yeah it must suck Nigel walked out like he did. Wake up and smell what you can have with me. But no . . . you'd rather soak in your own self-pity. I'm not a good enough person to feel sorry for you because the Brit walked out on you. Deal with it. Deal with your regrets, because I have none."

I grabbed my keys and left her standing there speechless. But seeing her hurt face before I walked out of her bedroom cut my gut open. I slammed the door behind me to make sure she understood I was pissed. The sad thing was it killed me to yell at her like that.

It had been hours since I'd left Tate standing there. That was the first time I'd ever had the last word.

In my bedroom, I lay on my bed, staring up at the ceiling. I reached for the picture frame holding the shot Matt had taken of me and Tate at Homecoming. When she trusted me enough to jump the rail and her breasts didn't want to stay tucked in her dress. The way Tate grabbed the top and pulled it up. I could still feel those breasts in my hands from earlier. She was perfect.

The intercom clicked on. "Zach?" my mom called.

I glanced down and I had a hard-on. *Think of Mom walking in and seeing it. Hurry. Go down. Go down.*

"Could you come here, please? You have a guest at the door."

A guest? I pulled the blankets back, and all was calm again. *Has a mind of its own.*

I stepped out into the hall and heard her voice.

"Sorry to interrupt your evening, Mrs. Bertano. I should have called first."

I stepped into the foyer. "Tatum?"

Tatum turned toward me and smiled. She took my breath away.

"Zach, I should have called first . . . you always do."

"No, it's okay. Don't worry about it."

Mom glanced over at me with a smile. She was thinking the same thing: a girl who comes to your house unannounced was one who was nervous about what she had to say.

My mom waved her hand around. "Tatum, don't worry. Nicola is working and I'll be in the office. If I don't see you again before you leave, it was a pleasure, my dear girl." Mom turned toward me and walked into the office and closed the door.

"Here, let me show you around the estate." Tatum

let me take her hand and I showed her everything
but my parents' room and their office. Only family
got to go in there. For security reasons alone. Out in
the backyard, we sat on the terrace furniture.

"It's stunning out here, Zach. It's so beautiful."

"Thanks. I'll let my mom know you like her gar-
den. So, what's up? Did Nigel call? Or come back
over?"

She played with her hand, tucked in between her
legs, and wouldn't look at me. Tate was really nervous.

"No. He didn't." She snapped her stare in my direction. "That's fine. Not that it would matter, but it
would be nice to talk to him. Anyhow, that's not why
I came here tonight."

"All right, why don't you tell me?"

She put her knee up on the cushioned bench and
faced me. "I'm sorry about earlier."

"Sorry? About what?"

"The way I talked to you and treated you like you
were the one who'd hurt me. And using you to make
me feel better. It was all wrong. And I'm sorry."

I grabbed her nervous hands and held them. "Relax.
It's fine. You'd know if I was pissed. And no matter
how pissed you make me, I would never hurt you."

Tatum gave me a quick but tender kiss on my
cheek. She looked out into the yard.

I whispered, "Would you want to go to my room
to finish our talk?"

Tatum nodded.

I took her hand and led her to my bedroom, down
a separate wing from my parents. "In here." I stepped
to the side. Tate went in and looked around.

I followed her inside and didn't bother her while

she studied my walls. She circled my room with a look of wonder. "It's so clean, your bed is made and . . . oh my gosh, Zach, who took all of these pictures of us? How many are there?"

"A lot. It doesn't freak you out? You don't think I'm a stalker or anything?"

She stopped and bit her lower lip. "No. Not at all. I'm assuming someone took these, since you're in half of them. Looks like an art gallery of the two of us on this entire wall. Oh my gosh. That's a lot of pictures."

"Not sure about an 'art gallery of the two of us'— there's definitely more of just you. Anyhow, Matt took most of them. I may have taken a few."

"They're beautiful." Tate resumed admiring the wall.

They were. They were beautiful pictures of her. It was a relief she didn't freak out seeing my walls covered with her face. I could see where most would freak out, but Tatum didn't. She always looked at situations with a different eye.

Tatum spun around to me with her eyes wide open. "Wait, these weren't out when Mariacella was here? Don't tell me she knows what I look like?"

"No. No. Mom helped me clear the room, and then when she left, we put them back up."

"Okay."

She walked over to me, eyes drooped. She was making me sweat. I wanted to touch her so bad. Her hand came up to my ear and stayed.

Her gorgeous eyes pierced mine. "Maybe I'm just as weird as you, because I think it's sexy. In a weird way. But I'm fine with weird."

"Sexy? Great. I'll take it!" I laughed.

"What's down the hall here?" Tate looked into the dim hall off to the right.

"Just my closets and the bathroom."

She stood there. "That's a lot of mirrors."

"They're just sliding mirrored closet doors. Looks worse than what it is."

"May I sit?" She motioned toward the bed.

"Oh my Go . . . sh. Of course, sorry." I had no clue why I was so nervous.

I sat next to her on the bed. "You seem like you're in a better frame of mind tonight."

"Maybe. I'm not sure I'm ready to talk about him again, but thanks." She looked up at me. "Zach, you know it's possible to be in love with two people at the same time. Right?"

"I think you can be, but there's always the one person who takes your breath away."

Her eyes popped wide open and her mouth dropped. What did I say wrong?

"You okay, Tate?"

"Yeah, just . . ." She paused. I could see her swallow. "I know what you mean. That's all." She glanced away. She wasn't comfortable.

Great. I was nervous and she was uncomfortable.

"I guess I should go." She moved.

I stopped her. "Stay. Please. We can watch a movie. Like we do at your house."

"Sure. Let me call my mom real quick and tell her I'll be later." Tate made the call.

I opened the armoire and Tate gasped. "Oh my gosh . . . you have your own entertainment center in there. How cool is that?"

"The question is what to watch?"

"No, the question is, why did we ever watch movies in my room when you had this state-of-the-art setup?" She laughed.

Just hearing her laughter made me want to kiss her. She had no clue how in love I was with her.

"Because you were scared to come to my house."

She lowered her head and looked sheepish. "I'm not scared anymore."

She knew how to make me ache for her.

"Anyway, next you'll pull out a couch to sit on?"

"No, just the bed, if that's okay?" I couldn't wait to get her scent all over my sheets.

"Gee . . . if this is all you have, I suppose it will do." She giggled.

Tatum flipped off her ballet flats and climbed in bed, grabbed a pillow, and stuffed it behind her back. I never wanted the movie to end.

"Okay, my suggestion is *Young Frankenstein* by Mel Brooks."

"Fine with me. My dad goes on and on about how genius Brooks is."

"You haven't seen this movie?" I grabbed the tape.

"I don't think so. Do you like old movies too?"

"Sure, who doesn't?" I shoved the tape into the VCR and turned around. She was staring off to the side, not saying a word.

I climbed in bed next to her. "Hey, you okay? You kind of went off to another place or something."

She shook her head and grinned, but I could tell it was forced. "Sorry. I'm fine." She wiggled in her seat, this time with a sincere smile. "Are we set?"

"Yup." I grabbed the remote from the nightstand and pushed Play. Then I hit the dimmer light switch on the wall, next to my bed. Tate shook her head. I couldn't help it if Bobby and Sergio could wire a house better than NASA.

As the movie progressed, Tatum scooted farther down in the bed. I followed her. When she jumped, I threw my arms around her.

She laughed. "Stupid me."

I didn't care she got scared, she was in my arms. Tatum got more comfortable, sliding over to me and resting her head on my chest. When Terri Garr rolled around in the hay, Tatum looked up at me with soft eyes.

"She's so pretty."

"Not as pretty as you." I pulled her closer to me.

"Zach, do you really love me? Are you getting this wedding called off, or do you want to marry her?"

Not that. Why would Tate take the chance of ruining our evening?

"To be honest?"

Tatum nodded, not taking her eyes off of me.

"If I could, I'd ki—" Tatum's body stiffened. "I will do everything I can to get this wedding called off. But if I don't, trust me, it won't last long."

Tatum swallowed and took a breath. "Okay, but I don't know what I'd do if you left me again."

"Tatum, just because I'm in Italy doesn't mean I've left you."

"No, promise you'll always tell me before you leave for Italy? Don't do what you did at the holidays last year."

"I promise."

She settled her head back on my chest, watching the movie.

If it wasn't clear before, it was now—how badly I'd hurt her when Gramps sent me to Italy like he did. I wasn't sure what got into me, but I felt it was time to be more direct with her. "Tate, not that it matters, but you know I'm a Bertano and since I spoke for you, that would secure your place in my family . . . once we . . . uh . . . once we're a couple."

"Huh?"

I exhaled. *Totally screwing this up with her.* "Whatever happens between us, I will not let Gramps know anything. I know you want to stay comfortably on the outside of the family, and I will honor that. You call the shots, Tate. Always."

She lifted up from my chest and titled her head to the side like Gizmo does.

"Tatum, I'll always be madly in love with you. Forever."

"Forever is a long time, Zach."

I held the side of her face. "I will always be madly in love with you, until the day I die."

"Forever?"

I didn't hesitate. "Forever."

"Oh, Zach. I love you too," she started crying.

Tatum moved up to my face and I met her halfway. I pulled her up and she slid over me. I could feel the tension in her lips. I wanted more of her and slid my tongue in her mouth and inspected every inch.

She felt so good I could have passed out if it weren't for my heart beating out of my chest. I grabbed her hips. They felt so good under my hands, I wanted to kill Nigel for being able to touch them whenever he wanted.

Tatum sat up and straddled my waist. "You've

always said it was my decision. And I'm making it my decision. But is this okay with you?"

"Anything you want is fine with me." Was she asking what I think, or pray she's asking for?

She grabbed the bottom of her shirt and pulled it over her head, exposing a black lace bra.

My jeans were so tight it was painful. *Oh God she's stripping.* Tatum reached back and unclasped her bra and let it drop. I couldn't breathe. Her beautiful breasts were staring back at me, waiting. She bent down and pulled my shirt off, her breasts almost touching my face. I'd died and gone to heaven.

I sat up and held her body to mine, and she wrapped her slender legs around me. "I love you so much, Tatum. Are we seriously going all the way?" I was going to come before she even got naked.

She held her mouth at my ear. "As far as I can feel . . . we are."

And we did.

Numerous times I had to think of something other than Tate's body, like spiders, to avoid coming too quick.

I couldn't believe this was finally happening with Tate. I didn't want it to end. And I never wanted this memory to falter. So I grabbed under her ass and carried her to the hallway and up against the mirrors.

I couldn't redirect my focus anymore seeing her breasts from every angle. They made me come without thinking.

I dropped my grip around her hips. We were both trying to catch our breath.

"Let me go take care of this," I kissed the side of her neck and pulled away from her.

I went into my bathroom. I grabbed tissue to dispose of the condom. *Crap. I didn't even feel that.* "Tate?"

"Yeah, I'm out here. Do you want me?"

I pulled the condom off and wadded it inside the tissue. "Yeah, there's a problem." I tossed the tissue and washed my hands.

"Yeah, what's wrong?"

I glanced over my shoulder. She looked so gorgeous. In my wildest dreams I never thought Tatum Duncan would be standing in my bathroom doorway butt naked.

"The condom had a split in it."

CHAPTER 17

Tatum

Monday, May 14, 1990

IT HAD BEEN A WHOLE week without hearing from Nigel. I was bound to fail every exam this week and the next. I couldn't focus. The question *Would it have mattered if I slept with Zach or not* kept going through my mind.

Another week and a half before I could sleep late and not worry about Nigel calling me. It seemed like the perfect summer break to me.

"Tatum?" Zach said, snapping his fingers by my ear to bring me back to him. "Hon, don't do this another week. Please?"

"Do what, Zach?"

"Tate, you go off to la-la land," Di said.

"Sorry. Did you say something?"

"No, just . . . look . . . I'm not sure if this is your way of punishing yourself. But do you think for one minute Nigel is doing the same? I guarantee you, he's not," Zach said.

I hated when he made sense. "Probably not. But

doesn't change my guilt."

"Oh my Go . . . I mean gosh," Zach looked like he bit a sour grape.

Di giggled.

He huffed. "Okay, I get your guilt, because of who you are. But stop torturing yourself. Because the sad fact is, he could have screwed someone else by now. I wouldn't put it past him."

"Just stop it. I don't care what he does. Doesn't change how I feel."

Zach got in front of me and pushed my back to the locker. His body cascaded over mine. "You should feel happy you found out now. Stop torturing yourself. If you don't, you'll force me to react, and you don't want me reacting to your tears. Trust me." Zach came down to my face and kissed my bottom lip and pulled. "*Inteso?*"

I hated when he spoke Italian, drove me crazy. "Yes, understood. I'll do my best."

"Okay, enough. The bell is about to ring, let's go," Di said.

At lunch, I stood between Di and Andi, pushing our trays along the lunch line. I glanced around to make sure a Bertano didn't walk up to us without my knowing. "Tell, me, Andi, what do you know about his plan? Is he getting this wedding called off soon?"

I wasn't about to continue anything with Zach if he was lying to me.

She glanced around us. "All I know is Bonita, Tyler's girlfriend, is keeping them updated. Zach calls her a lot to get info about his fidanzato and whether she's cheating."

I glanced at Di. She quickly looked away. She was

thinking the same thing I was. Maybe Andi didn't know about me and Zach. Maybe for once a guy in my life, kept his word and wouldn't tell the family right away. Of course, it worked out in his favor not to tell, because he would be guilty of cheating too. It could mean my head on the block if that psycho Mariacella found out, though. Maybe sleeping with an engaged guy wasn't the best idea. She could come after me, but I did ask for my actions to only have consequences for me. Suppose this was what they mean by *watch what you wish for.*

"Well, not sure how that's going for him, but he keeps saying he's going to get it called off. I don't know. That's his problem. I need to learn not to worry about things I have no control over."

Di patted me on the back. "Now that sounds like a good plan."

CHAPTER 18

Zach

Wednesday, May 23, 1990

OUR LAST LUNCH TOGETHER BEFORE the summer break began, and I was the only one in the school who didn't want it to end. When the last bell rang, I would have to focus everything I had on getting out of my wedding the next month. Mariacella kept sending me pictures of the venue and the flowers. Her excitement didn't make sense, because she had made it clear to me she was only marrying me to inherit her father's vineyard. She didn't know her father had signed a contract saying I would manage and own his property upon our marriage. Her name was nowhere on the deed, the will, or the contract. Her father knew once Mariacella got ahold of it, she would sell the land and blow the money. Like Gramps, Mr. Davide wanted to protect his family for years to come. Couldn't say I blamed him.

What I cared about more was how Mariacella had been an angel, but Bonita swore she didn't know of anything she did wrong. There was no way in hell that whore kept her legs together. Either my fiancée knew we were onto her, or she was sneaking around the back.

In less than three hours, that would have to be my main focus.

Not great timing considering Tate and I had smoothed everything out the past week. She'd finally realized and accepted how much I loved her, even if it meant just being the lame shoulder to cry on because that Brit never reached out to her again. Nigel had her wrapped around his damn finger. But he clearly wasn't in it for the long haul. It didn't make me feel great, but I didn't walk away because she'd slept with him. Every time that thought crossed my mind, my body quivered from head to toe. He'd had his hands all over her.

Temper. Control your temper.

"Zach? Hello . . . Zach?"

I snapped back to the now. "Sorry, Tate." I reached over and kissed her cheek. She blushed.

"So, are we still on for Saturday? I'm soo ready to get out and do something besides studying for exams and worrying about guys breaking my heart."

Yeah, me too . . . "Sure. I'll get ya at noon. Be ready . . . you'll be out of the house all day. A movie, shopping, and more. So much more."

She laughed. But what caught my attention was the dirty look Di kept giving me. She could stay sore. Tate and I were staying together whether she and her boyfriend, Tommy, liked it or not. Tate was moving on with me, not Nigel.

"Good. Surprise me, but I'll be ready. Can't wait. And Di and Andi, you guys still spending the night tonight?"

"I am," Di said with a wiggle of her ass. That meant she had something up her sleeve.

"Me too, I'm looking forward to a girl's night," Andi said.

Of course Matt gave her a crooked look. He was so possessive of her. I wasn't sure why. Andi didn't go out with the girls like she used to.

Tate and I walked to our locker alone while the others stayed back. She grabbed the last of her books and made sure the locker was empty.

"Just three more hours, Zach. Then we're out of this hell box." She closed the locker door and leaned her back against it. Her eyes drooped, and she sighed.

"What is it?"

"*He* used to call this the hell box."

I leaned against her. "Tatum, it's natural to say the same things." Nigel was there every time I needed to talk to her, he always somehow made an appearance. "It gets better, trust me. Look . . . I need to let you know that this summer I have to go back to Italy to get things worked out."

"When?" Her beautiful faced turned down.

"Don't worry. In a couple of weeks. Just for a few days, a week at the most." I couldn't tell her it was next week, not yet.

"Oh." She glanced away for a moment. "Are you sure you're getting this called off? I can't keep doing this if you're engaged. I just can't, Zach. It's wrong we did it in the first place."

I pulled her into me and squeezed. "Baby . . . I mean, hon . . . don't worry. I promise you I'll make this work. I swear."

I leaned down and kissed her lips. God, she felt good, so warm and soft. I wanted to run my fingers in her long blonde hair and tangle my hand in there so we could never part. I looked forward to taking her out Saturday night. I wanted nothing more than to be with her on a real date. We hadn't done that for six months.

This was what I'd waited for. To win her over. And I'd won.

CHAPTER 19

Tatum

Friday, May 25, 1990

DI PICKED ME UP AND was driving us to James-town Mall.

"Okay, so out of your whole closet, you can't find anything to wear tomorrow for your da . . . date"— Di shook her head—"with Zach?"

"Look, saying it is not a dirty word. Jesus. You think this is easy for me? I loved Nigel. But I haven't heard from him since Prom. It's been two weeks."

"I know. He's not talking to Tommy about you anymore. Suppose he fears Tommy will tell me and then I'll tell you. And he's right."

Di parked at the center entrance and we walked into the mall and headed for Dillard's. They weren't as busy as they'd been for Prom dress shopping. That thought kept Nigel in my head. I'd been so excited to go to Prom with him. We'd had a great time until . . .

"Tate, how about something like this?"

Di showed me a blazer. I had a blazer to match almost everything I owned. "You think I need another one? How about a skirt? Or a dress? I never wear skirts anymore." Of course Di had no clue why I'd stopped wearing them. Since the day Kyle raped me, I'd stopped wearing miniskirts. Then I'd started dating Zach and wore them again from time to time.

Di and I worked up an appetite finding the perfect outfit for the next day, so we headed to our favorite mall restaurant for dinner. Sipping on iced teas always felt good after shopping.

Di rubbed her stomach and bent forward. "These stupid cramps are killing me. I wish I'd just start this period and get it over with."

I stirred the tea with my straw. "Gosh . . . I feel like I haven't had a period in forever."

I noticed Di sat still in her seat, her eyes frozen from fright. I whipped around to see if Kyle had walked up behind me. Nothing there. I turned back around. Something popped me upside the head. "What did I just say?"

"Uh, Tatum?"

I haven't had a period in how long? Oh no. Oh no. My body began to sweat. The room had gotten warm in that it sent my sweaty palms to my thighs and every pore on my body flooding. "Di, we need to leave. Now."

She flagged our waitress down and got the check. "Tatum, when was your last period?"

"Di, I don't know." I grabbed my pocket calendar out of my purse and flipped to last month for my big ink dot. "This can't be happening."

"Just look. Hurry."

I searched every single day in May—nothing. I flipped to April and found a big ink dot. "Found it!"

I thanked the Lord. "April first was the day I started my last period. Wait . . . that was . . . Di, that was nearly eight weeks ago." I looked up at her. "We need to go to the drug store. Now."

"Maybe you're just late." Di meant it to be taken as matter-of-fact, but it came off like a question.

"No, I'm clockwork."

"Are you on the Pill?"

"No," I huffed. "You think my mom would let me go on the Pill?"

"Well no, but some girls take the Pill to stay consistent. It even helps to control cramps."

"Nope, not me. Suffer through."

We tossed money down on the table and left. She drove straight to drug store.

We walked in together. "Okay, glance around for me. Tell me if you notice anyone. I don't want someone I know to see me buying this."

We were in and out in a few minutes. I sat in the passenger seat of her car, staring at the box that could put a major kink in my life plans. They claimed to be able to tell me sooner than the other brands if I was pregnant or not. But they suggested I do the test in the morning, first pee.

"I can't do this tonight, it has to be done tomorrow morning. Di, I can't wait that long."

"You'll have to. You want the most accurate result. I know you're scared, but don't freak. Maybe you're not and you just need to go to the doctor."

"So let's hope I have something else wrong with me? Geez. What options I have."

"What time is Zach getting you tomorrow?"

"He said noon."

"Okay, take the test in the morning, first pee, and then call me the moment you find out. If I don't hear from you by eleven, I'm calling your ass."

"Okay." I couldn't take my stare off the box. I felt her hand pat my shoulder.

"Tate, it'll be okay. I'm sure you're not. You said you used protection every time."

"Yeah, every time." I turned my head to her. "But with Zach, it split." I held my breath, waiting for her to yell at me.

Di's eyes went golf ball size again. "Tatum, tell me you're kidding?"

I couldn't breathe. I slowly shook my.

Di took the palm of her hand and smacked her steering wheel. "*Damn it,*" she yelled out.

I could feel my world crashing around me. I stood in the trash compactor like in the movie *Star Wars: A New Hope*, with the walls closing in on me, and all I could do was scream.

"Tatum, pray you're not pregnant. Pray."

"Well no shit, Sherlock, but why are you so pissed? It's my life going in the crapper, not yours."

Di took a deep breath. "Because they will keep the baby." She looked me right in the eyes. "Makes no difference what you want in life. Gramps will own you." She put her arms over her steering wheel and dropped her head there.

"Nooo," I yelled at the top of my lungs. Then the tears came spewing down like a dam being opened for the first time. "I hate myself. Why did I do that? One time and I'm pregnant?"

Di sat up and wiped her eyes. "Try to get some sleep. Tomorrow is going to be rough if that shows up positive."

"No shit, Captain Obvious." I grabbed a tissue out of my purse and blew my nose. "Thanks for being here for me, Di. I hope this doesn't change our friendship?"

"Of course not. You may need me sooner than later." Di pulled me into her. "Love you. Call me in the morning."

"Love you too. Night." I got out of her car and waved goodbye from the side door.

I tiptoed across the floor and got ready for bed. I never imagined myself with a baby, and couldn't. No matter how bad it was being broken up with Nigel, life wasn't so bad. Junior year has ended and we would be starting our senior year soon. I couldn't start school back up pregnant. How would I go to college? I couldn't. But an abortion? No. No way. I didn't want a child, but I couldn't abort one either. No. I couldn't live with myself. Always wondering what the baby would've turned out like. Would the child have been a boy or girl? This wasn't the baby's fault, it was mine. The baby shouldn't have to pay for my mistake.

Then again, the test could turn out negative. All of the worrying and debating would not matter at all.

The last thing I remembered that night was crying against my pillow . . .

Hearing my family shuffle around and slamming doors woke me.

"Toni, go to the car and tell your dad I'll be right out."

"Okay, Mom."

A banging on my bedroom door made sure I was awake. My mom opened up and popped her head in. "Tatum, wake up. We're leaving. See you when you get home tonight."

"Sure."

Mom closed the door, and a moment later the front door slammed shut. They left. I felt terrible, my body ached. I lay there in bed for a moment and I could feel the trash compactor closing in again. I had to hurry and take the test.

I hopped up and grabbed the drugstore bag from the back of my closet, opened the box, and grabbed one of the pregnancy sticks. On my way to the bathroom, I glanced at the digital clock on my night-stand—ten thirty. Plenty of time. Even though I was home alone, I locked the door. I read through the directions once again and prepared the stick and held it underneath me. The whole time I peed, I prayed more than the Pope.

Please God help me out this one time. I swear I won't ask for anything again if you make this negative. Please.

I finished and put the cap back on, waiting for the single or double lines to show up. Within seconds, the double pinkish line began to appear. Something was registering. Come on, single line. I was worse than a gambling addict at the poker table. *For the love of God, give me a single pink. Please.*

The double pink line was strong.

Maybe it didn't work. Maybe that was why they gave you two pee sticks. I tossed it into the trash bin and ran for the other test stick in the box. A few min-utes later, it too showed double pink lines.

No. No. This can't be happening.

I washed my hands and took my pee stick with me to the bedroom. My hands shook so bad I could barely dial the phone.

Di must have been waiting for my call because she answered on the first ring. "What did it say?"

"It said, can you come over? Now." I hung up. Just in case someone else at her house picked up the phone, I didn't want them to overhear. Di had to know what it meant.

I paced my bedroom so fast my feet ached. I couldn't be pregnant. This wasn't how life was supposed to turn out. I wanted to go to college. Grandma left me money in her will for college tuition. All I had to do was get accepted and pay for books and living expenses. I could be whatever I wanted. Not now. Not if this test was right. *Oh my God . . . why did I do that?*

Someone banged on the front door. I ran and flung it open. It took everything I had not to bawl my eyes out in the doorway, but I didn't want a neighbor seeing me respond to Di standing there and tell my mom.

I pulled Di inside and slammed the door shut. We went to my bedroom and locked the door. I spun around to face her and flashed the pee stick.

"*Positive*," I yelled.

Di grabbed it and turned the stick sideways to read the window. She looked up at me. "You have to tell Zach when he gets here."

"Di, what if I don't? What if I somehow got an abortion? Could you drive me?"

"Tatum? Do you know what you're asking? What

that would mean?"

"It means I would be aborting this chil—" I couldn't finish before the crying fit began again.

Di flung her arms around me and squeezed. "Jesus, Tate. I'm so sorry."

As if I needed anything else going on, my stomach churned. "Di, I need to lie down."

"Geez . . . you're changing color. Here," She moved her purse off the bed and straightened my pillow. "Lie back. You could be in shock."

"I'm not in shock, but I feel like I could throw up." When my head hit the pillow, my stomach did a back flip. I sprung out of bed and ran for the toilet.

Di was right behind me and shoved the toilet seat up in time. She grabbed my hair back. "Jesus Christ . . . what did you eat?" She reached over and flushed because my insides were coming out all at once.

I was exhausted when my stomach agreed I'd had enough. I flopped down to the floor and my back against the tub wall.

Di got a cold, damp cloth for me. "Tatum, I should call your parents. You should go to the hospital after that. Do you have Sprite or ginger ale?"

"Di, I can't tell you my name right now, let alone what's in the fridge." I wanted to sleep. Answering her put my exhaustion level over the edge. I rested my head back on the tub ledge. "I just need to rest for a minute."

"Do you feel better? Maybe it was food poisoning? *Or* morning sickness."

I forced my eyes to open and look at her. "No, there's no way I can go through that every day. No way."

There was a knock on the door and it opened. Di ran out into the hall and huffed. She ran back in and mouthed, "Zach's here."

Maybe I should have just let my head drop in the toilet. That would have been more pleasant than telling him he was a dad. I wasn't sure if I could handle having a baby. This was my decision, not his. And God knew after that I did not have the energy to fight with him.

I could hear Di say, "Zach, she's sick."

His boots hustled across the floor, getting louder. "What's wrong?"

Zach appeared in the doorway. I focused on him. He was so sexy. And I looked like death resurrected wrong.

He dropped on the floor next to me. "Tatum, do you need a doctor? I'll take you right now."

Di stood behind him and cleared her throat. I looked around Zach at her, and her eyebrows were arched upward. She was saying, *Tell him now.*

I was afraid to tell him. This was my choice. We didn't agree on a lot of issues. And I didn't want his Gramps to control me.

"Tatum, hello? Do you want me to take you to the doctor? You look like you need one."

I turned to his caring eyes. He always said everything was my choice. This was his opportunity to honor his words. But damn it if I didn't want to trust him. If I didn't have an abortion, soon, I would have to tell him anyway. He, like the rest of the world, would know. Having my back against the wall was my own fault.

I took a deep breath and didn't take my eyes off his.

"I'm pregnant." I held my breath.

Zach's face twitched and then froze. "What? What did you just say?"

"You heard me. I'm pregnant."

Zach examined my body from head to toe, twice. "Really? The child's mine?"

"Well, you're the one whose protection . . ." I felt the tears gathering in my eyes. If I blinked, they would fall.

Zach smiled and put his hand on my cheek. "You're pregnant? Are you sure?"

Why did the asshole look happy? "Di, could you get the stick?"

She went to my bedroom and came back holding the evidence in her hand. "Here. Double lines means pregnant."

Zach took the wand and turned to the window, like Di had.

His mouth spread into a beautiful bright smile. "It's true." He jerked his stare in my direction. "Tatum." He tossed his arms around me and pulled. "I love you."

I pushed him away. "Stop. It hurts." He let go and kept one hand behind my back, but looked at me. "And I'm not sure if I'm keeping this pregnancy. I have a decision to make."

"You? Don't you mean us?"

"I mean, I'm not ready for a child, but I'm not sure I can abort one either."

He narrowed his eyes and turned to Di. "Do you agree with her?"

Di flung her arms up. "Whoa, I am out of this. I'll do what you need, but this is Tate's decision."

Zach came back to me, his beautiful smile gone. "Don't do that, Tate. You'll regret it your entire life."

"I have no life if I don't." If that didn't make me sound selfish, I don't know what did. The thought of going over to Illinois for an abortion broke my heart. I would be eliminating this child's potential. Their life. My head was killing me.

I flopped my head back on the tub ledge again. "This can't be happening."

"Here." Zach pulled me to my feet.

I made a pit stop at the sink to clean up. When I finished, he continued to help me to bed.

"Lie down."

I did and after a while I felt better, but still queasy. Di sat near my feet and rubbed them.

"Look, I will take care of you—"

"I do not need taken care of."

"I will help you. My family will."

"No. I don't want your family to know."

Zach dropped his head. "Tatum, this child is mine." His stare met mine. "I will be involved. Even if this child isn't mine, I will be involved. I love you, Tate. I'm not going anywhere."

Why did hearing him tell me no matter what, he wasn't leaving me make me want to cry worse than I did watching Julia Roberts die in the movie *Steel Magnolias*? Didn't he know showing a broken woman support had a terrible effect on her? Asshole.

I reached up and he met me for a kiss.

His smile was back. "I love you."

"Oh Zach, we need to think about this. Really. I mean, my family—"

"I want to be here to tell them. I will do the talking."

Now he had a death wish.

"Okay, I will say this." Di paused. Zach turned to look at her. "Tatum's parents will freak. Especially her mom. Her dad will punch you. I mean, the guy was a boxer. Punching guys is fun to him."

Dad was going to murder Zach. He needed help talking to them.

"Tatum, I'll go tell my parents, but I'll wait to tell Gramps . . . although . . . this would help."

"How in the world would this help you?"

"Bertanos never turn their backs on blood. This child has Bertano blood, you're golden. My only problem is that I cheated on Mariacella, but I'll work out that detail."

You're golden . . . you're golden . . . Zach said that to me before. If I spoke for him, I would be golden. "What about this baby, are they golden too?"

Zach giggled with joy. "You can only dream how golden this child will be. Yes, this child is golden."

That sounded appealing. Too appealing. There had to be a catch. There was always a catch with Gramps.

"Look, the moment I tell my family, you get whatever help you want," Zach said with too much excitement.

"Okay, seriously thinking . . . what about the hospital bill? Doctor visits? I would go every month. That gets expensive. I'm on my dad's insurance, but I'm sure it doesn't cover a birth. I don't have money. I would need diapers, formula, clothing—"

"Paid for, paid for, paid for, and worked out. Besides you won't need formula, you'll breastfeed."

And so it begins. "How in the world will I breast feed in school? In case you haven't noticed, not many girls have newborns on their breasts in class." This whole idea of doing this sounded worse by the minute. This wouldn't work. I couldn't do what he expected.

Zach looked so happy, I was beginning to get mad. "Stop smiling. Can't you yell at me or something? This will cramp our lives."

"First, I don't like yelling at you, but this will not cramp my life. My family will help us. That's what we do."

"You just have this all worked out, don't you?"

"It can be if you let me."

Zach got that look. The look I couldn't resist. He flipped off his boots and crawled into bed with me. Di crawled in on my other side and stared up at the ceiling, ignoring us.

Zach wrapped his body around mine. "No matter what happens, I'm committed to this child, too, forever." He kissed me. Kissed me for the first time. He didn't let go while his tongue dug deeper. I held his head to mine. Sad, but I wanted him to make me feel better, and his kiss did the job.

I backed away and took a breath. "Okay, tell your family. If it will help you."

"Tate, the wedding will be immediately called off."

"Positive?"

"Positive. This will only be good news to my family."

"Sorry, but it won't be to mine."

He caressed my cheek. "I'm sorry. But I will help every way I can. I promise you that."

Zach was good about keeping promises like that. Maybe I could trust him.

"Okay, tell your family today. I'll tell mine tonight.

But you need to be here to help. My mom scares me when she's pissed."

"Scares me too," Di chimed in.

Zach looked over at Di. "Are you going to stay with her? If you are, I'll go talk to my family now. Otherwise I can take her with me."

"*No,*" I yelled.

Di chuckled. "No, I'll stay." She glanced at me. "I've always said she's going to need me."

She was the best friend anyone could ever hope for.

Zach gave me a kiss and got out of bed. "Okay, I'll be back by five. Call if you need something before." He put his boots on.

"I'll be fine. I'm already feeling better. Like it's passing."

"Thanks for helping, Di." Zach bent down to me and cradled my face. "We'll be fine. This won't be the end of your world. I promise you that."

The sentiment was beyond sweet, but not possible.

He walked out.

After we heard the door shut, the doggie door flapped and then Gizmo's claws on the floor came closer. He trotted into my bedroom and joined Di and me on the bed. He lay against my stomach and dropped his head there.

"Di, when my parents get home, all hell will break loose. You may just want to go home. Protect yourself, don't be in the line of fire."

"I'll survive. It's you I worry about."

"That makes two of us. If I get dressed, will you take me to get a late lunch?"

"Wherever you need to go. Get dressed. And toss this." She flashed the wand.

"Yeah, we'll put it in my nightstand for now."
Not sure why I was saving the proof.

CHAPTER 20

Zach

THIS WAS THE HAPPIEST I'D been since we'd slept together. Then before that, when she said she would be my girlfriend. I couldn't get home fast enough. I sped into the driveway and slammed on the brakes and ran into the house.

"Mom? Dad? Come here quick. I have good news."

They came running out of the office. "Zacharia, why are you home? What happened with your date with Tate?"

"Take a seat." I pulled out a dining room chair for Mom.

She sat. Dad looked skeptical. I paced the table in front of them.

"When I got to Tate's today, she was over the toilet, throwing up."

Mom smacked her hand over her mouth. Her eyes brightened.

I stopped pacing and faced them. "She's pregnant! And the child is mine."

Mom jumped up from her seat. "Hallelujah, Zacharia. Nicola," Mom tossed her arms around my dad.

"It was Tate I saw pregnant. Tate."

"Yup. And now we can tell Gramps to call off the engagement with Mariacella."

Dad wasn't as excited as Mom and I were. "Okay. Okay, you two. I admit this is good news, but not for everyone. Sit down, Zach. We need to discuss a few things."

I grabbed a seat and hit it hard. "Yup. I already told Tate I will be there tonight when she tells her parents. I will take full responsibility."

"Son, that's admirable, but your dad is right."

"Zach, Mariacella will not be happy. Which means we will have to deal with her and her father. He wants protection. This marriage guaranteed that."

"Right. Let's get Gramps on the phone then. Then let's call Italy. I have to be back over at Tate's at five to talk to her parents."

Mom reached over the café dining table and patted my hand. "Shall I go over with you and talk to Tate's mom?"

"I'm not sure. How about you be on standby? If things get out of control and I need reinforcement, I'll call you."

"Deal." She sat up. "Zach, Tate agreed she's keeping the baby?"

"How did you know she fought—"

She cocked her head to the side.

"Never mind, stupid question. Anyway, she wasn't sure. She's scared and fears her life is over. She didn't say that straight out, but I could tell that's what she's afraid of. But we talked about it and then I let her know she wasn't alone, and I would be involved, no matter what. I'll just have to dig into my savings to help."

"Zach, Mom and I will pay. Don't worry about money. This will be the firstborn great-grandchild, so Gramps will contribute. Now . . . to call him."

The three of us went into his office and got Gramps on speakerphone.

"Ciao, Nicola."

"Gramps, I have Cat and Zacharia with me on speaker, and we have some exceptionally big news."

"*Dillo* (do tell)." You could hear him take a puff on his stogie.

"Zach, tell your Gramps," Dad said.

"Hi, Gramps. Tatum is pregnant with my child."

"*Coas* (what)?"

Mom leaned toward the speaker on the desk. "That's right. Zacharia is expecting his firstborn child."

"Dis is very good news. *Complimenti!* We must call dis wedding off. You will marry your Spoken For and make the child legitimate."

I turned to Mom and Dad and whispered, "No, Tate will freak worse if I rush this. She won't agree. I know her."

"Uh, sure, Gramps. In time. Let the girl tell her parents she's with child first. But Tate will speak for Zach, soon."

I nodded at Dad. He saved my ass there.

"Fine. Let's call Mr. Davide and get this resolved now."

I swiped my forehead, not realizing I had begun sweating.

In a matter of minutes, we had Davide on three-way speaker.

Gramps greeted him and didn't beat around the

bush. "My friend, we must call dis wedding off between Mariacella and Zacharia."

"Oh, dis not good news, Bertano. *Come mai?*"

"Why? Because I am expecting my first great-grand-child."

"No. No. I need protection. You guaranteed protection."

"I guaranteed protection once they married. They won't now."

"I need protection. You know my situation, Bertano."

"I'm sorry, but my blood comes first."

He wanted protection and now with Tate's pregnancy, he wasn't getting any. How much was it worth to him? I motioned to Dad. He leaned into me. "Dad, see if he gives me the vineyard as payment for protection?"

He backed away and smiled with a nod. Thank God he liked the idea.

"Gramps, if I may, there's maybe one way we would agree to protection."

"Nicola, what is it?" Gramps asked.

"Sign over your vineyard, Davide, to Zach and his firstborn as payment. Then you'll get your protection."

"Nicola, son, that is a reasonable offer. Davide, do we have a deal?"

"I think it's fair. But you know it's nothing but dirt, Bertano?"

"We know, and so does Zach. He agrees," Dad said.

"Grazie, Zacharia. Mariacella will be broken-hearted, but I thank you."

"I will fax over the contract and you send it back

signed. Then send the deed to your vineyard's property in Zacharia's name to us."

"Done," Davide said.

We hung up with Mr. Davide, but we stayed on with Gramps.

"Zacharia, now you go tell this German's family. You move to Italy after school and you marry your Spoken For."

"Gramps, I would be honored to. But first, both of us need to complete our senior year here and then we can move forward. This will be a relief to Tatum's father, I'm sure."

"Perfetto! I will let you know when the deed and contract get here. Zacharia, you have made me very proud of you. You tell thees girl's father we will pay for everything. We take care of our own."

"I will, Gramps. Thank you."

We hung up with Gramps and my mom grabbed me for a bear hug. "Zacharia, this is fabulous. You get Tate, a baby, and a vineyard for our family." She backed up and held my shoulders. "You have made us all very proud."

Dad came over and gave me the supportive father hug. "This will be a new beginning for our family."

"But we still have to have protect Mr. Davide's family over there."

"True, but Davide won't live forever," Dad smiled.

Mom clapped her hands together. "Let's have a drink and toast." Mom ran out of the room.

I glanced back at Dad. "Am I supposed to take your comment to mean anything besides the obvious?"

Dad patted my shoulder. "No, son, just none of us live forever. Especially ones with cancer."

We joined Mom in the kitchen and she poured a shot of brandy. "Zacharia, I know you don't drink anymore, that's why I poured just a shot. You have a child on the way. Stay sober now more than ever."

We each took a shot and raised out glasses.

"Son, your mother and I can't begin to tell you how much this means to us that you have the first-born in the next generation, and you will one day soon set us free. We love you."

"We love you, Zacharia!" Mom raised her glass higher.

We all called out together, "Salute." Then we tossed the shot back.

Mom prepared a celebratory lunch. The three of us sat down over food and discussed future plans for me and Tate with the baby—Italy after graduation—the vineyard—working on getting Gramps to accept the family's desire to change businesses for good.

I looked at the clock. "It's four thirty. I better get ready to head back over. I need to brush and gargle before. Tate will smell that one shot a mile away."

My mom laughed. "And now that she's pregnant, her senses could be even stronger."

CHAPTER 21

Tatum

"THANKS FOR DRIVING ME AROUND for a bit, Di. I feel better after getting some food in me."

Di had driven me to lunch and then the mall to return the outfit I'd gotten the previous night. If I was keeping this baby the clothes wouldn't fit for long, and I didn't have money to waste.

"No prob. I think you needed to get out for a bit too. Get some fresh air. You know, your parents should be back soon and you'll have to deal with that."

"It's quarter till, Zach should be back too. He can talk his way out of anything."

"Tate, I'm going to tell you this, but trust me when I say, I know it makes no difference now. I just thought you should know."

Di pulled up in front of my house, parked and then turned to me. "Nigel called Tommy last night and asked how you were doing. He also asked if he, or I, thought you would see him. I won't tell Tom about your pregnancy. That's your place."

If Nigel knew I was pregnant with Zach's baby, he

wouldn't want to see me.

"Obviously your situation has changed and I won't be telling Tom what's happened. Just that you prefer for Nigel to not contact you. If you want to see him, you'll call him."

"Thanks for letting me know. I appreciate it."

We got out of the car and walked up to the house. Di was more than a friend to me, she was a sister. She understood me and supported me like only a sister could. I loved her very much.

We walked into the front door. The moment the door closed behind Di, my mom yelled, "Tatum, come here. Right now."

I turned back to Di and whispered, "I can't even get in the door before she's calling me."

Di stood frozen with bulging eyes. I whipped around and a hand smacked me across the face. I went flying into the coffee table.

"Oh my God, Tate." Di dropped to the floor behind me.

I took my hand to my forehead and rubbed the dent where my head had collided with the table, then examined my fingertips for blood. They were clear.

"*What the hell is this?*" my mom yelled.

I turned back to her and she flashed the pee stick. How did she get that? I put that in my nightstand. Ugh, my cheek burned.

"Cindy, what is going on?" Dad came running up from the basement. "What fell?"

Toni stood in the hallway crying. "Daddy, Mommy knocked Tatey down. Hewp her."

Di grabbed under my armpits and pulled me upright.

My mom became Mr. Hyde. Her pupils were tiny and her eyebrows arched. "I found this pregnancy test in the bathroom trash. You're pregnant?"

Dad turned the corner into the living room and noticed Di helping me to my feet and ran over to grab me. "What the hell, Cindy. Did you knock her down?"

My mom shoved the pregnancy stick in his face.

He took it. "Tate, is this yours?" He looked at me, his faced drained of blood.

"Dad, please listen. It is—" I sat down on the couch. My head hurt.

Dad shot a dirty look at my mom. "We can be pissed, but don't you lay a hand on my daughter again."

Di hid in the front corner by the door, whispering on her mobile. I couldn't hear who she was talking to.

Poor Toni sat in the doorway crying.

"Tone, come here. I'm okay," I waved for her to come to me.

She ran and sat next to me. I patted her back. Gizmo barked in the backyard and then ran through the doggie door flap. He joined Toni.

"How could you go and get yourself pregnant? Who's the father?"

"Well, Cindy, I assume it's Nigel. They've been dating for months."

"Dad, we broke up at Prom."

My mother flung herself around and began erratic pacing. "My daughter is not having a baby out of wedlock."

"Tatum, who is the father?" Dad gave me a daring

eye.

"Zach is."

Mom and Dad glared at each other.

Di closed her mobile and joined me on my other side. She whispered in my ear, "He'll be here in two minutes. He's pissed."

My dad was going to punch Zach, and Zach would not stand there and take it. I felt nauseous again.

"Ken, get the car. We're taking Tate to Illinois right now."

"Whoa, wait . . . an abortion?"

"What else?"

"Cindy, I am not driving my daughter to get an abortion. You're not thinking straight."

"Daddy, make it stop. Mommy's mad."

Dad picked Toni up. "Cindy, stop yelling. It's scaring Tone."

"Then take her out. I need to talk to Tatum."

Dad looked back at me. I gave a slight nod. It was better to not traumatize my little sister; I could stick up for myself if need be. The truth was, I would never have struck my mom, no matter how violent she got with me.

He took a deep breath and walked outside with Toni. "I'm taking her over to your parents' house. I'll be right back. And I want to talk to Zach, Tatum. ASAP, tonight. Get him over here."

"He's on his way."

"Good. As soon as I get back I'm talking to him, man to man." Dad closed the door behind him. "Toni, stop crying. Tatey is fine." His voice was muffled.

Mom stepped up to me and pointed her finger in my face. "You tramp." Before I could duck, she smacked me across the face.

Di jumped next to me. I held my cheek. It was burning worse than a second-degree sunburn and felt split. I kept checking for blood.

"I will not be a grandma. I'll drive your skinny ass over to Illinois myself. No daughter of mine will have a baby before marriage."

"Mrs. Duncan, I know you're upset—"

"Diane, do not get involved. This is not your business," Mom warned her.

I stood up. Easier to block a hand coming at your face. She wasn't going to touch me again.

"Yes, Mrs. Duncan. That's true. But Zach will be here any minute to talk to you."

"To me? What does talking do? Nothing. Is he going to take care of this baby? Pay for its medical expenses? Insurance? Clothes? Food? Housing? I think not. He got what he wanted." Mom turned her fury back to me. "How could you think it's okay to spread your legs for a boy?"

I'd had enough of her breaking me down, and I knew all too well that was what she did to people. Insult. Insult. Insult. Until you ended up not caring and she got her way. Well, not me. Not this time.

"Maybe it's not okay that I spread my legs, but at least with Zach I felt real love. That's more than you've ever shown me."

My breath caught. I'd gone too far. I could see her hand going up again. I turned, bracing myself for the third-degree sunburn. It didn't happen. I slowly opened my eyes and saw Zach holding my mom's arm back.

"Sorry, Mrs. Duncan, but you're not laying another

hand on Tatum."

Mom stumbled back. "What? What are you doing? Get your hands off of me."

Zach let go of my mom and waved for me to join his side, not taking his glare off of my mom. Di got on his other side. Zach held me to him. "Now that I'm here, I'd like to talk to you and Mr. Duncan, please. Is he home?"

"He left with Toni," Mom shot back.

I looked up at my savior. "She was upset with the fighting and he took her out. He'll be back."

"All right. Shall we sit and wait for him to talk?"

"Who the hell do you think you are, coming in my house and ordering us around? You got what you wanted. But I'll tell you what . . . Tatum isn't having a baby."

I could feel Zach's body tense.

"Mrs. Duncan, I understand this isn't the best news to you. But I plan on taking care of Tatum and my baby. My whole family will."

"You know, that's a problem too . . . your family. Over my dead body will I allow lawbreakers to take Tatum away from me."

I could feel Zach thinking that was possible. "Mom, let him talk. No one is taking me away."

"That's right, Mrs. Duncan. I will support this child, financially and in every other way."

"Huh . . . you kids think it's easy to just have a baby and because of love everything will be fine. Well, I'll tell ya . . . love doesn't pay the bills."

"Mrs. Duncan, I said I plan on taking care of this baby and Tatum, and I mean it."

"I've had enough . . . Tatum, get in my car. I said

you're not having a baby."

Mom grabbed my arm and pulled me toward the door. Zach grabbed my other arm but then let go. I could see his struggle of not wanting to pull me in the opposite direction. I couldn't do anything but swallow the bile back down.

"Mrs. Duncan, please. No. We'll work this out. I'll move her in with me. Just stop. They're not even open on a Saturday night."

Di stood there covering her mouth, tears running down her face.

My mom grabbed the door handle. "The hell you will. She's getting an abortion. Tonight."

I was afraid to force myself away from my mom for fear of hurting her. But she had lost her mind. My mom flung open the front door.

She gasped and came to a halt. "Uhh, what?"

I looked up and saw Catalina standing in the doorway.

She looked radiant as ever with her beautiful smile in bloom. "Good evening. I'm Catalina Bertano. I'm this baby's grandmother. May I come in?" She pulled the screen door open and walked right in, never waiting for a response.

Catalina stared my mom down with an ice-cold glare. "Mrs. Duncan, I presume?"

My mom dropped my hand. "I don't believe this. What do you want? Hasn't your son done enough?"

Zach pulled me away and nodded at his mom in response.

I said a Hail Mary. Cat was going to cream my mom.

"Mrs. Duncan, let's use first names. We'll soon be

family. Hi, Tatum, dear."

"Hi, Cat." I couldn't look at her for the death glare my mom was giving me. If she felt more threatened, she'd kill me later.

"The hell we will." My mom crossed her arms tight over her chest.

"I'm sorry we don't agree. That's unfortunate. Zacharia, why don't you and Di take Tatum outside to get some fresh air? Di, go get Tatum's purse." Cat gave a gentle nod.

Di hustled past my mother.

"Excuse me, this is my house." Mom snapped her head from Di to Catalina.

"Mom, I'll be back. Need air. Talk to Catalina."

Zach held me in his arms and hurried me outside.

"When you come back, you're getting an abortion," my mom yelled.

"Mrs. Duncan, that is truly an ugly word, something I cannot and will not allow to happen to Tatum and my grandbaby."

I could hear them from the driveway.

Zach shoved me in the back of the Suburban. I hopped in the back row and took a seat.

Matt was driving. He glanced back at me. "Hey, Tate. Congratulations!"

"Thanks, Matt. But now is not the time." Didn't they see this wasn't the best news?

Zach hopped in next to me. I noticed Di running out of the house with my purse.

Bobby sat in the middle row looking out the window and up into the house.

"What's going on here?" I asked.

Bobby held out his palm, and Zach dropped his car

keys in them.

"I'll see you guys back at the Manor. Catwoman is coming out now," Bobby said, jumping out of the Suburban.

Matt snapped to and shifted, ready to drive away.

I listened in. I could hear my mom yelling, "How dare you threaten me. Do not come back in my house again. I'll do whatever I want. That's my daughter."

"Yes, I understand Mrs. Duncan. Goodnight. We will be in contact."

Catalina jumped in the front seat. "Mattea, drive now."

My mom slammed the front door shut.

I turned to Zach, and he looked about as terrible as I felt. "Oh, Zach."

I dropped my head to his shoulder and let the two slaps across my face be a reminder of my mom's hatred of me. I had never been so afraid in my entire life than I was at the moment.

My heart beat against my chest, reminding me I was alive. The back of my neck and my hairline were moist. How did my life go from carefree mall shopping to having a baby and an unstable mom taking her anger out on me in less than twenty-four hours?

He rubbed my back. "Shh, hon. It's over for now."

"Tatum, where was your dad?" Catalina asked.

"Ken took Toni over to her grandparents' house because she was scared," Di answered. "Cindy knocked Tatum down the moment she walked in the house. Poor Toni saw the whole thing. She was rightfully scared."

"Cat? What's going on?" I asked.

Catalina didn't turn around to me. "You're staying the night at our house. Cindy is irrational and insists on an abortion." She turned back to me. "And *that*, I swear on my life, will not happen." She turned back to face the front. "So until I, or someone, can talk some sense into her, you will not be going back home. My grandbaby will not be aborted."

"No, you're right. This baby won't be. But I need Gizmo. And I can't leave Tone alone with Mom."

She glanced back at me. "They'll be fine. She's not pissed at them. Just you. You disappointed her."

"Story of my life . . ."

Zach squeezed me to him and kissed the side of my head. "We'll go to Tyler's manor. He lives there alone."

"Zach, we need to talk in private."

"Okay, when we get there. He's setting up your room."

"My room?" I was an inch from Zach's beautiful face.

"Hon, you'll have a permanent space in our family."

"I'm not sure I deserve that." I stared into his eyes. In them was a promise to me and this child nothing could break. "I think I love you, Zach."

His dark eyes gazed back at me. "I know I love you. And that baby."

He pulled me in for a forever kiss.

CHAPTER 22

Tatum

WE ARRIVED AT TYLER'S HOUSE, and he opened the door and let us inside. He didn't take his eyes off of me when he said, "Tatum."

"Tyler."

Zach pulled me past him, as if he owned the place. I wasn't sure how Tyler felt about Zach and me invading his home. I didn't know how the family felt about firstborns, and this would knock him and Bonita out of the running for Lead positions. I bet Tyler hated us.

Catalina led us to the living room sitting area, with floor to ceiling windows in an A-frame ceiling, overlooking their *Better Homes and Gardens* backyard.

Zach sat next to me on the couch.

Cat took a chair. "Tate, is there anyone in your family that you can talk to? Anyone besides your mother, someone who can side with you? Not your father, he'll be in the middle enough as it is."

"I haven't spoken with her in a while, but my Aunt Matilda, Aunt Mattie. She's my dad's sister. Mom used to be close to her."

"She'll work just fine. You need someone else from

your family in your court. Give her a call tonight. For now, you're staying here. Do not go back home. Your mother is adamant about an abortion. Tatum, listen to me." Cat leaned forward and didn't blink. "This child is not to be aborted. You could leave Zach, but the child will remain. Is this understood? We will support you and this child for life. No matter what happens between you and Zach."

For life? I didn't have to marry Zach and the baby would still be taken care of? "I guarantee you, Cat, I don't want an abortion. I'm keeping my baby. But what will I owe you for this help?"

Zach took my hand. His cousins stood around the living room, witnessing, it was clear by the way they stood there—hands behind their backs, not staring at us.

"Nothing. You owe us nothing but this child's life."

"Neither I nor this child will be under Gramps's control?"

"I hope one day, in the near future, you would marry my son, but no, you won't be under Gramps's control. If this child is a boy, he will be raised to be a Bertano, though."

"I don't want this for him."

Zach helped control my shaking hand by squeezing.

A gentle smile spread across Cat's face. "I understand, and so does Zach. That's why he has secured a vineyard in Italy. Maybe one day you'll move there with him and run the vineyard as yours. But a new business, a way out, is what your pregnancy has brought us. The child will not be aborted. We all have Zach to thank for this way out."

Catalina only moved her stare, not her head, behind me—Tyler.

Zach secured a vineyard? How?

"With the announcement of your pregnancy, a deal has been made to get us out of the old business, and the new one is an operational vineyard."

"Doesn't look like a bad deal, does it," Catalina asked.

"Not at all. I would love to work and own a vineyard with the whole family." I glanced around the room, and Matt, Bobby, and Di and smiled. Standing behind me was Tyler, and he didn't share an expression.

"Call this Aunt Matilda, and I'll get dinner. The others are coming over, so be prepared." Cat stood.

"Sorry. Who is coming over?"

She glanced back at me. "Your family, Nicola, Piero and Maria, and Sergio. Zach, show her to your room."

"To your room?" I whispered in his ear.

"The guest room. It's the only one on this floor. I'm staying with you tonight."

"Why? Why can't we stay in your room at your house? It's big enough."

He glanced at random features on my face with a soft grin. "We could, but this would keep you closer to home and Di. And I'm staying so you don't feel weird being here alone with Tyler."

"I see. You guys have this all figured out pretty darn quick."

Zach led me down the hall. "It's what we do."

I was glad they weren't leaving me alone with Tyler, This was his parents' home, and he didn't look thrilled I was pregnant.

We walked into a cozy room with a queen-size bed, two nightstands with a lamp on each, and a chair in the corner. Spacious, but nothing spectacular.

"Tate, can you take that side? I like being near the window if that's okay."

"Fine by me, whatever you prefer."

"There's the phone." He pointed to my nightstand. "Feel free to call your aunt in here."

"Is it tapped? Are you going to be listening to me?" I wasn't a complete fool.

"No. There's an intercom on the wall." Zach nudged his head to a small white box on the wall by the door. "We won't listen. I promise."

"Can you have Di come in?"

A few minutes later Di walked through the door.

She shut the door behind her. "All I will say is, this isn't that bad of a deal."

"Oh, shut up. Who wants to be pregnant their last year of high school? And no plan for college? Now will you stay in here while I call Mattie?"

"Of course." She took the chair in the corner.

I took a deep breath and dialed. If she agreed with my mom, this was going to be a quick phone call.

Aunt Mattie answered right away.

"Hi, Mattie? It's me, Tatey."

"Hey, Tate. Where are you? Your dad called me."

"At a friend's."

"Okay, so let me tell you first and foremost, I will not side with your mother on this. She is absolutely out of her mind right now."

I glanced up at the ceiling. *Thank you, Lord!* I mumbled under my breath.

"Why are you surprised to hear me say that?"

"Huh? Oh, well, you never know for sure on something like this."

"You knew or you wouldn't have called. Anyhow, your father got to me before you did and asked for help."

Out of the corner of my eye, I could see Di watching my face. I gave a nod, confirming Auntie was in my court.

"Anyhow, your parents are beside themselves that you're not home. Your mother made it sound like you were kidnapped by this boy's mother. Tell me about him. But tell me first, what happened? Why did this boy's mother show up? Was it really to talk as a new family?"

"I was not kidnapped, dear Lord. I left to get some air after Mom smacked the crap out of me and sent me flying into the end table."

Mattie gasped. "She hit you?"

"Yeah, twice. That's why Dad left with Toni. Poor thing saw it happen. I'm fine, but she smacked me a second time after Dad left. Anyhow, his mom came over to stop Mom from taking me over to Illinois, and to talk about future plans for the baby. But you wouldn't believe some of the things she was saying to me."

"Like what?"

I explained everything that happened to Aunt Mattie.

"Wow, really?"

"Yeah, let's move on. His name is Zach and it kind of happened. We didn't mean to, it was an error . . . anyhow. His mom is just a strong-willed woman. Nothing wrong with that."

"No, nothing wrong with that. So, obviously Cindy neglected to mention any of that to your father. But no worries, we'll get this worked out. Cindy's always been the irrational, flying-off-the-handle one."

I felt like saying, *No shit, Sherlock.*

"So, Tatey, how else can I help you?"

"Can you tell them I'm sleeping at a friend's? And see if she'd keep her mouth shut to any of my friends' parents. I want to give everyone the chance to tell their parents before they hear through the grapevine. And could you please change her mind, Auntie? I'm not having an abortion."

"Hold on, I'm writing this all down, but go back to the third request and repeat that one again. You were going a little fast there."

"Whatever. Okay, which one again?"

She chuckled. "Joking, I got it all. So, I'll call Cindy and talk to her and your dad, but she doesn't know he's called me. Now, tell me more about this boy. Do you love him?"

The hardest question to answer, because I was in love with Zach, but we were complicated. I was afraid of what that meant—a life in the Mob. "I do love him, and have for a long time. They're Catholic Italians, they're a close-knit family—"

"I can forgive the Catholicism. Is he tall, dark, and handsome?"

"Geez . . . yes, but does that matter?"

My aunt laughed. "You bet your skinny ass it does. Ahh . . . I do love me a tall, dark, and handsome Italian. Anyhow, I went off somewhere else, continue please."

"Anyhow, his mother, Catalina—"

"Cindy couldn't remember her name. But mentioned to your father how arrogant she was. Continue."

"Well, I would if you'd let me."

"Oh, man . . . I haven't seen you in such a long time." Aunt Mattie laughed. She took a deep breath in and took her time exhaling.

"Auntie, are you doing your cards? Stop! Anyway, I was saying, Catalina told Mom off and I ran for it. So there." I could hear her flipping her tarot cards faster than I talked.

"I'll call Cindy now and talk to her about the long list you gave me." She busted out laughing. "How could you be my sister-in-law's child? You should have been mine."

I should have been any other female's in the family but for my mom's. The moment Di saw me hang up the phone, she stood.

"So all went well?"

"Yeah, she's going to call my mom and knock some sense into her. Hopefully tomorrow will be better."

"It should be. I hear the others getting here, so you'll need to go out."

"After that, I really just want to take a bath and go to bed."

"I bet you're pooped. Just put face on for them. Don't let them see you weak, Tate." Di put her hand on my shoulder and made me look her in the eye. "Never let them see you weak, and feeling you can't do something."

What Di said hit a nerve, an old nerve in my gut. The one I'd shut down when I first fell in love with Zach. Something had told me for weeks that there was something different about him, something, warning me to not get involved. Then again, the day he came back to St. Louis and I had dinner with his family and fiancée, I was forced into a Mob dinner that could have ended very badly for me.

I wouldn't show them any weakness. Ever.

After taking a deep breath, I straightened my back. "Let's do this."

Di and I walked out in the hall, and the noise got louder and louder.

Andi popped in the doorway. "Tate? Oh my gosh, I can't believe you're pregnant." She forced me to walk backwards into the hall. She leaned over to my ear. "When did you and Zach? You've kept a lot from me."

"Not really, just that. But if you must know, the night after Prom."

"Before you go out there, I'm just going to say, everyone but for one is ecstatic about the news. Suppose you're smart enough to realize who?"

It wasn't rocket science. Tyler was the only one who didn't speak to me. "I figured. Anything I should know before I walk out there?"

Andi stood before me, squared off, and held my shoulders. "Hold your head high." She stood to the side and let me pass her.

Di stayed at my side and Andi pulled up the rear. We stepped out of the hall and into the family room. The women in the kitchen and the men in the family sitting room stopped what they were doing and stared at us. Everyone except Tyler smiled.

I would have to watch him. We girls stood there, and I held my head high but didn't know what else to do.

Zach ran over and took my hand. "You have no clue that you're already taking your place. It just comes naturally to you."

I kept a grin on my face, with everyone still watching us, but whispered to him, "What? And why are they looking at me like that?"

"How did you girls walk out here?"

"You're not making sense. With our own two feet."

"You led them. Andi pulled up the rear, just like Mattea and Piero does. Di's at your side, just like Sergio is with my dad."

I'd be damned if I did what they do. I turned around to Di and Andi. "Can you guys go stand somewhere else?"

Di huffed, "Ungrateful." She walked over to Bobby and climbed on his lap.

Andi chuckled. "Hormones kicking in already." She walked over to Matt.

I looked at Zach's self-righteous smirk. "Don't say a word."

He laughed and put his arm around my waist, leading me over to the others.

After dinner, Catalina set up the hall bathroom as mine. It made me uncomfortable that she made everyone use the upstairs hall bathroom. No one complained. I just didn't like being the reason for the change in habit.

Catalina placed an armful of soaps, scrubs, shampoos, and conditioners on the double marble vanity. "Here, set this up in here the way you like. It's yours. Take your time."

Cat turned to walk out, but I grabbed her arm. "Cat, a minute, please?"

"Is everything okay?"

I made sure to not take my eyes off her. "Sure, everything is fine. I need to thank you for all of your help. I'm not sure how today would have ended if it weren't for you and Zach. I'm grateful. And so is this child."

Catalina held her lips together in a beautiful smile and pulled me into her chest with a gentle squeeze. "My dear, you are *so* welcome." She let go and held my shoulders, bending down to me a little. "I know you and Zach are young, but I look forward to the day you speak for him. I've always wanted a daughter, and I couldn't have asked for better."

Those words went straight to my heart and warmed me. I hugged her. Catalina was the mom I'd prayed for. And if I could get it in my mother-in-law, then so be it.

Catalina closed the door with Di and Andi in there with me. Andi began organizing the cabinet. Di stood there.

"You know I don't need all of these products." I started the water in the double-person soaking tub. In my mind's eye, I could see Nigel and me back in his tub, soaking with bubbles up to our chins. So much had changed in the past month.

"Tatum? Hello?" Di patted my back.

"Sorry, what?"

"You tell me. You're the one staring down at the water."

I undressed and stepped in. "Just thought of something. That's all."

Andi continued to arrange and load the cabinets, while Di sat on the toilet seat. "Tommy called during dinner. I called him back and he knows something big is happening. But don't worry, I didn't say a word."

After all this time, Di still kept her word and didn't tell Tommy about what she was dealing with. I'd hit the jackpot with her friendship, because what girl doesn't confide in her boyfriend over news like this.

"I don't want you to lie for me, but it's probably best to keep this on the down-low for a while longer."

"Uh, yeah," Andi snickered. "I heard the guys talking about canceling their graduation party. They don't want to call any attention to us right now. Not until you get this squared away with your parents and they get the whole Italy thing taken care of. Can't believe Zach got Davide's family vineyard. She's going to kill him."

"I feel like killing him. The one time and the stupid condom splits . . . really? Didn't he feel that?"

"So that's how it happened." Andi sat on the floor next to the tub. "I won't say anything, but they're all taking bets how it did. Of course, they're all wrong."

Di shook her head. "Yeah, that's Zach and Tate's business. Keep that quiet."

"I can't believe it. Why me? Why now? It's not just me I'm taking care of, I'll always be responsible for another life." The acorn was lodged in my throat, my chest expanded, and my skin felt hot. One quick blink and the tears fell.

"That said . . ." I sniffled and held them back. "I can't do what I originally considered. I can only imagine the emotions I'd endure if I got an abortion. The torture of never knowing. Maybe having the baby is more selfish, because I'd fear the daily *what if* question. Does that make sense?"

Di and Andi nodded.

"We all know how much I enjoy the unknown."

They snickered.

"I can't live not knowing what will happen to this child. So why me?"

Di looked at me. "Tate, to be honest, I always hated this saying, but it applies to your situation. God gives us what we can handle. Stupid. But if any of us can make this work, it's you. But why? I don't know. Maybe it was meant to be. Sucks. But maybe?"

"You sound like my grandma." That reminded me of one of the last things my grandma had told me before she died. "*Fight for what you believe in. There's always a price to pay when you want something bad enough, or something honorable. If there's anything you take from me, fight for what you believe in. Always.*"

Did she know? How could she have known this would happen to me? Of course, the way she played with tarot cards and taught Aunt Mattie, naturally she "saw" this would happen.

"Keeping the baby is the right thing to do. I'm ready to fight for her, or him. The hand I was dealt sucks the big one, but what's done is done. I'm ready. With Zach's love, I can do this. Then if the Bertanos say they'll help us, they will. It's not where I wanted to be, but I'm trying to look at the bright side . . . this gets Zach his vineyard and the rest of the family out of the business. I'll just have to pull my weight. I just hope not too much."

I turned away from my bubbles and toward Andi and Di. Their glassy eyes and genuine smiles made me snap out of my rant. "If that makes any sense?"

They moved toward me, arms out.

"Group hug." Andi chuckled.

"No, I'm all wet and naked."

"That's not stopped us before," Di laughed.

CHAPTER 23

Zach

EVERYONE LEFT TATUM, TYLER, AND me alone. Tatum was in bed reading her favorite book, *To Kill a Mockingbird*. I walked in the bedroom and locked the door. She ignored me. Her foot was tapping. She was nervous.

"Tomorrow will go better. Once we go over and talk to your dad, I'm positive you can safely go back home."

"Wish I had your optimism." She snapped her book shut and put it on her nightstand. "I'm just tired. Been the longest day of my life."

Tatum sunk under the covers and pulled them up to her chin, and wasn't so subtle about watching me walk to my side of the bed. Guess she liked the view. The feeling was mutual.

"Are you wearing more than boxers to bed?"

I grabbed the covers and hopped under. "I can wear less if you want."

She giggled. "Zach!"

"What? You've seen it all before."

"It was dark . . ."

"Tatum, are you flirting with me?" I lined my body against hers. She smelled of heaven—lavender and vanilla. My groin acted on its own free will again.

Tatum snapped her head at me. "Uhh, happy to see me?"

I slid on top of her body, bearing my weight on my arms. She seemed to notice.

"I am. You're the only thing that makes me happy."

Sunday, May 27, 1990

Tatum wouldn't stop playing with her hands during the drive over to her parents' house. "Just stay at least an arm's length away from Dad. I'll worry about Mom."

"Tatum, your dad isn't going to punch me. I'm more worried about your psychotic mother, to be honest." I patted her knee. "Remember, I'm doing the talking. Just sit there and look pretty."

"I will slug you myself if you say another sexist thing like that again."

Her anger was so cute. She would slug me, and it would hurt, but I would totally deserve a good punch. Tatum was capable of taking care of herself.

I parked in front of her house. Tatum looked around the neighborhood. I ran around to her car door and gave her my hand. When she got further along, getting out of the low-sitting car would be hard for her. Guess I'd have to buy a family car next. I'd do anything for her.

When we got up to the porch we heard Gizmo going crazy.

"The neighborhood knows we're here now." Tatum chuckled.

She opened the door, and Gizmo leaped for her arms. "Ohh, Gizzie. Did ya miss me, boy? I missed you."

Toni joined Tatum's side and whimpered, "Tatey, you can't weave again."

Poor Tatum had the dog and her sister giving her a guilt trip. I grabbed Toni and picked her up. "Tone, let Tate in the door."

We stepped in the living room and her mom came hustling around the corner. "Toni, back off."

This woman tested my patience. I patted Tate's shoulder to let her know I was right there. "Hey, Mrs. Duncan. Is Mr. Duncan here?"

"I'm coming," Mr. Duncan called out. He was hustling up the steps.

"So you got everyone on your side. Well, I'll tell ya what . . . I'm not giving you a damn dime for this baby."

Tatum dropped her head and looked away.

"Cindy, don't start. I want to talk to them before you chase her off again." Mr. Duncan walked into the living room and took his recliner. Tatum sat on the far end of the couch, away from her mom. I sat next to her, keeping me in between them all. Toni and Gizmo climbed up in Tatum's lap. It was clear Toni felt more safe with Tatum than her own mother.

"Zach, why did you have unprotected sex with my daughter?"

A punch would have been a better way to start this off. Tatum started choking and turned every color of the rainbow. I patted her knee to let her know everything was under control.

"Mr. Duncan, I didn't. There was a . . . a . . ." I glanced at Toni. "A technical issue."

"Ken, is that important?" Mrs. Duncan huffed.

"Yeah, it is."

"Toni is in the room, change the subject," Mrs. Duncan growled.

"Fine." Her dad shook his head. "What's your plan?"

I glanced at Tate. The color in her face was coming back. For the first time, I understood Tatum's anxiety about talking to her parents. Her dad was fine, but with her mother setting the tone—which was horrific—the suffocating environment sent my nerves to the meat grinder.

"I'm going to take care of everything, sir. And I don't want Tate to have an abortion."

"Well, I agree with you there." He glanced at Cindy and narrowed his eyes. "My mother would roll over in her grave if I let my daughter, especially Tatum, have an abortion."

Cindy gave him an equally dirty look and then sulked.

He looked back at me. "So we're on the same page there. Now, what about school? You're to finish."

"Yes, sir. I will. So will Tate."

"Then how do you plan on taking care of her?"

Mr. Duncan was losing his patience. No wonder why Tatum had none with parents like this. "Sir, my family has agreed to pay the financial part until we graduate. Any babysitting or anything like that, my family will take care of as well. Trust me, this child will be cared for. And if you prefer, I can move Tatum, and the baby when the time comes, in with me."

"See . . . told you they think this is so easy. That's what his mom was coming in here saying."

Mr. Duncan looked at Cindy. "What is your problem? If they want to contribute so much, let them."

Tatum patted my knee this time. I glanced at her and remembered what she said, that her mom must have control over everybody and everything. If my family stepped up, Cindy would lose all control. She didn't want Tate, but she didn't want anyone else to have her either. I was starting to get a good dose of what Tatum had been dealing with her whole life.

"They're not taking my daughter away."

Mr. Duncan shook his head. "You are impossible." He looked over at us. "Tatum?"

She popped her head up. "Yeah?"

"Do you want to live here or with Zach?"

"I want to stay here, but I don't want to worry about the next time I'm getting knocked down or yelled at. I feel crappy enough as it is."

Mr. Duncan turned and pointed at Cindy. "You touch her again, and you and you and will fight. I want my daughter home."

Mrs. Duncan stood up from the loveseat. "She can come back home, but I'll be damned if I give her any money." She stormed off.

"No one asked you to, Cindy. Go in your room and pout like a big baby." Mr. Duncan rubbed his balding head. "If it's not you aging me, Tatum, it's your mother."

"Dad, I'm sorry. I don't know what to say."

I would run away if I had to grow up in this family. Tate was a good person; this didn't make her bad.

"This shit happens. Just wish it didn't happen to my

daughter."

"Mr. Duncan, I'm happy to move Tate in with me and my parents. They already said they'd make a room for her."

"No, Tatey. You stay wif me." Toni squeezed Tate's neck.

It wasn't even my family and I could feel the tough situation Tatum was in.

"All right, Tone. I'm not going anywhere." Tatum squeezed her little sister.

"Zach, son . . . I have your word you're going to financially help Tatum and your baby?"

"You have my word." I looked into Tatum's beautiful blue eyes. She took my breath away. "Sir, you have my word. I'll start by taking her to her first doctor's appointment."

Tatum took a deep breath and smiled at me.

I had to look away. "If there's a bill sent to the house here, just hand it over and I'll take care of it. But I'm hoping I can pay as we go."

Mr. Duncan looked around. He leaned forward and kept his voice down. "Now, she's"—he nudged his head in the direction Mrs. Duncan took off—"Worried about your uncle's run-in with the law, but you keep Tate out of that. You hear me?"

"My family is well aware of that, sir. She isn't involved and won't be. I promise you."

He sat back. "Good. Sounds like we have an understanding. At least for now. I'm not saying we won't help out, but if your family is agreeing to bear the brunt, then that's fine with us. The missus will calm down. Once she gets a look at that baby, she'll come around."

"Sir, no disrespect, but if Mrs. Duncan hits Tate again, I'll move her in with me, no warning. And so you know, when Tatum and I graduate next spring, Tatum and the baby are moving in with me, no matter what."

"Well, she doesn't say it, but the missus and I appreciate your being honorable. Of course, you did knock my daughter up."

"Jesus." Tate ducked her head.

I understood her dad had to get the last jab. Because it was true.

"Speaking of being honorable . . . do you plan on marrying Tate after graduation, then? Make the baby legitimate?"

"I'm not getting married. Not for a long time." Tate looked back and forth between her dad and me. I could have told him her reaction to that question. I wasn't sure why he looked surprised.

"I would marry her today. But no matter what I want . . ." I stared Tate in her blue eyes. "She makes the call. Always."

Her face relaxed and she smiled at me. That look. That smile. I had to turn away again.

"All right, sounds like you two have this under control for now. Brace yourselves. It's not easy. Sounds good until the time comes and you have a baby with colic who can't sleep, and an exam in the morning or work." Mr. Duncan stood. "Guess it's time to get the shopping done." He put his hand out. "Thanks for being honest with us, Zach."

I stood and shook his hand.

Her dad took his time, but stared at us. "You kids can do this. Zach, be there for her. Hormones of a

pregnant woman are unpredictable, and Tate's young
. . ." He patted my shoulder. "You're going to need a
lot of patience."

He stepped away. "Toni, go get your crybaby mom
and tell her I'm leaving. She better be in the van in
two minutes if she's going shopping."

Toni ran off. "Daddy, Barbie needs another pair of
shoes. I wost them again. Bye, Tatey. See you waiter."

Mr. Duncan yelled out, "I told you to glue those
things on."

When they left, the house felt somewhat normal
again. Gizmo stayed by Tatum's side and we went
back to her bedroom. Tate stood there, looking
around. "Seems weird to be here now. Like it's not
home anymore." She glanced back at me. "You know
what I mean?"

I put my hands on her hips. "Say the word and I'll
take you and Gizmo back to my house."

She dropped her head.

I felt bad. The struggle was painful for her. "I can't
leave Tone. And I can't take her too."

I pulled Tatum into me. "Your call."

Their house phone rang and Tatum looked at the
caller ID window and then whipped her head at me.
"It's Nigel."

Tate didn't need anything else to deal with. "Answer
it."

Tate's shoulders raised and fell. "Hello?" She sat
down on the bed, next to the nightstand.

I wished I could hear what he was saying. If he was
going to start calling her again, I would have to tap
the phone.

"Nigel, now is not a good time. I mean . . . there's

not much for us to work out. At this point all I can hope for is a friendship."

I could breathe again. She was giving him the *let's just be friends* bit. He must be trying to get back together with her. Ha. He wouldn't want to if he knew she was carrying my baby.

"Things are kind of crazy right now. I appreciate you wanting to explain more what happened between you and Sam that night, but it doesn't matter now."

She puffed. "I mean, it's been over two weeks. Things change. A lot can happen in two weeks." Tate spoke softly, she sounded tired. "If you're going to get mad at me, I'm hanging up. And what I do isn't your business. The jealousy between you and Zach is something I'm done with. Again, thanks for calling, I do appreciate it. But I can't meet up right now." Tatum dropped her head. "Thanks. You take care too." She paused, blowing out a hesitant breath. "Nigel, please."

Tate looked back at me, and her eyes warned me she was on the verge of crying.

My chest felt tight. Was he making her cry for a bad reason or a good one?

Control the temper.

"Bye, Nigel." She hung up.

"What?"

She took a deep breath. "He still wants to try to work this out between us, even though I slept with you. He says he loves me more than anything."

CHAPTER 24

Tatum

Friday, June 1, 1990

FIRST THING MONDAY MORNING, I called my mom's OB-GYN and got an appointment. It was a good thing they had a cancelation for Friday or I could have waited another three weeks.

Zach picked me up and drove me to the doctor's office. "I just don't see why you couldn't go to our doctor, if I'm paying the deductible on this."

"Zach, it's the one thing I could give my mom to have control over. Let me go to him for now. I can switch later."

"At least she's been better this week."

"Yeah, she avoids me but I am A-okay with that. Better than knocking me across the floor."

He pulled into the parking lot and parked. He took my hand and walked me into the building. I wasn't excited, but I was glad one of us was. He took everything in stride. Zach really was the best for my nerves, he could say nothing and somehow calm me down.

We went into the medical suite and Zach stepped

up to the check-in window. "Tatum Duncan is here for her eleven thirty appointment."

"Go ahead and fill these out. We'll call her back shortly." The receptionist placed a clipboard with a book of papers through the window.

I grabbed the clipboard and a pen and began writing down my medical history, which wasn't much. "Jesus, do they need all of this?"

"Just fill out the top form about your personal medical and I'll do the rest."

Zach patted my knee and glanced around the waiting room. We were the youngest ones in there. A few people were staring at us, but I noticed Zach sat straighter. He was so proud. I was lucky to have him.

When I finished the first two forms, they called me back.

I stepped up to the nurse. "I only have these finished."

"No problem. That's what he needs the most."

Zach stepped up. "Can I finish the others while I wait?"

The nurse grinned. "That would be great. Here." She handed him the clipboard. "After the examination I'll be back out to get you. You both can talk to him in his office."

Zach gave me a soft kiss on my cheek and went to sit down. The nurse took me down the hall and we stopped on the scale.

She led me to their hall bathroom and instructed, "Pee cup and wipe. Wipe front to back first. Put the lid on and then put it in the window there. I'll meet you out here when you're done." She handed me the frosted medical cup.

I didn't screw around. I wanted this visit over with as soon as possible. My skin felt warm and stretched, and I noticed sweat beads forming around my hairline. I had to get out of there before I needed another shower.

The nurse escorted me to my room and shut the door behind us. "Okay, so I'm assuming this is your first visit to a gynecologist?"

"That's right."

"You know what he's going to do?"

My armpits felt moist. "I fear."

She grinned. "You're not the only one who dreads this." The nurse turned around and reached up into the cabinet and grabbed a large napkin. "Undress, from head to toe. He needs to do a full examination."

She handed me the oversized paper napkin. Did I need to blow my nose?

"Wrap this around you after you undress."

What? That wouldn't cover my head.

"He'll have you up on this table and put your feet in the stirrups."

She pulled down two stainless steel "footrests" connected to the end of the table. They looked right out of a Conan the Barbarian movie.

"He'll examine you vaginally—"

"Excuse me?"

She snapped her stare up at me. "He needs to check you vaginally."

What the . . . He sticks his hand up there? For the love of God . . . how was this for medical reasons? I pulled my shirt away from my armpits.

She patted my shoulder. "Don't worry. Doctor O'Connell is gentle."

Oh, thanks. Stupid me. What am I worried for then? I mean . . . I would have walked right out of here if he wasn't gentle.

The idea of walking out wasn't looking so bad. They couldn't make me do this. Was an examination necessary to have a baby?

"He'll listen for a heartbeat, and then you can meet Zach back in the doctor's office to get your due date and all of that fun stuff. Wait for him up on the table. He'll be in in a moment."

She shut the door on her way out.

That Witch . . . the fun stuff . . . my ass. I think she enjoyed her little demonstration. Torture the young girl . . . yeah, really funny.

I started stripping down, everything on bottom first.

When I was naked, I grabbed the napkin and gave it a gentle shake to open up. It was smaller than my mom's tablecloth. *How on God's green Earth does anyone wrap this around themselves?*

He was going to walk in and my ass would be facing him. I had to hurry and cover myself. I wrapped the napkin around my body the best I could. Got it. I was covered. Mummy-wrapped, but my ass wasn't exposed. Victory!

I stepped over to the barbaric "table" and took a step up and carefully turned around. Just barely bent back to the table when it happened. My ass popped out of there. The mummy piece of napkin ripped right in the rear, vertically.

"Stupid piece of . . ." I growled and ground my teeth so hard it was giving me a headache. I loosened the paper and readjusted. I pulled it up to my thighs, like a mini, strapless dress, and then it loosened. I slowly sat back down . . . and now it just ripped at the waist.

Did they have air conditioning in the office?

I swiped under my hair.

A knock came at the door. "Tatum?"

Doctor O'Connell stepped inside and closed the door behind him. He stood in front of me with his hand out. "Hi, Tate. Haven't seen you in about what . . . seventeen years? I had just started in my practice when you were born."

My mom thought it was cute to have the doctor who delivered me, deliver my baby. I didn't. "Almost eighteen."

"All right, let's see what we have here." He flipped through my paperwork. "Last period was April first or so?"

"Yeah." I took a deep breath. Did he think it helped to calm a woman to talk before he examined her? News flash, Doc, let's get this over with.

He continued to skim the papers and then put the clipboard down on the sink counter. "All right, let's see this little critter."

"Sorry? Critter?"

"You're pregnant. Positive showed immediately. Why don't you sit back and put your feet in here?"

He pointed to the cold, sterile "footrests." There was nothing comfortable about this. Couldn't they come up with something by now to make this easier on a woman? I had to lie on my back, spread-eagled so he could see my girl? Stupid.

I'm all ready for you, in all my glory. Because this piece of crap you supplied me with to cover myself doesn't work anyway. So please . . . be my guest.

He put his back to me while he snapped the gloves on. I wanted to take those gloves and smack the hell out of him instead.

I lay on my back and put my feet in the air. It took me forever before I let Nigel see my girlhood. *This doctor just walks in, says hi, and then I'm to spread-eagle for him?* My palms were wet. I had to be sweating through the napkin.

I looked up at the tile ceiling and didn't focus on what was going on between my legs. Because if I did, I would have snapped my knees closed on the doctor's head.

"Tatum, can you scoot your tush down for me?"

"What?"

"Tatum, I need your bottom closer to the edge."

I ground my teeth but scooted. Now my girlhood was closer to him, *like he needed to get a better look.*

He then moved something and made a clicking noise. I raised my head up and looked down at him. The doctor had a frickin' spotlight on my girl. "I'm killing Zach," I grumbled under my breath.

"Is he the father?"

"Yes, but he may be the deceased father soon."

Doctor O'Connell thought Zach's demise was funny.

"Okay, let's do the ultrasound."

That didn't sound so bad. I would get to hear the baby.

I glanced down and saw a long rod-like instrument coming down at me with a rubber sheath, and lube on the tip.

"What is that?" And how would that fit? It was

longer than my body. There was no way that would all fit. I thought an ultra-sound was with a wand like instrument they rubbed around your stomach.

"Your baby is so small, it's the only way we can see the wee one. Especially if you're only a few weeks pregnant."

I flopped my head back and took a deep breath. "Go."

"Don't be nervous. Be still, but breathe."

Well, that's easy for you to say. Let's have you in your birthday suit and let me shove a rod up ya. With all your manhood in my face.

"Breathe through the pressure." The doctor inserted the rod. "Breathe, Tate."

On the exhale, I heard a beat. Faint. But there.

That had to be the baby's heartbeat. The sound of my child's life, coming in my ears and going straight to my heart, made my body weak and my chest hurt. The baby was an extension of me. Another life was attached to mine. Oh my gosh. This made it so real now.

Everything I'd gone through the past month—fighting with Nigel—finding out I was pregnant—fighting with my mom—accepting I would have to deal with Gramps sooner rather than later—all came resting on my chest. But none of that mattered. What did matter was doing what I needed to do for this child. He wasn't going anywhere, he was fighting. I would too.

Tears slid down my face. I discreetly wiped my cheek. I wished Zach weren't missing this.

"Tate, you okay?" Doctor O'Connell asked.

"Yeah. I will be now."

"All right. We can't tell what the sex is yet, but you

have a strong one." He stood there holding the rod in one hand but kept his attention on the ultrasound monitor. "Almost done. One more thing to measure." With his free hand, he clicked on the mouse and made x's on the edges of the kidney bean looking shape. That's' my kidney bean. My child.

I knew how far along I was. Two more days and I would be exactly four weeks pregnant. I'd never forget the night Zach and I first made love.

He clicked once more on the computer type keyboard. "Okay, by the size of the baby, you're almost nine weeks along. *Congratulations, Tate!*"

To be continued . . .

D EAR READER,

I realize that where I *paused* this story may be a "barbed-wire pill" to swallow.

There are a couple reasons why I broke this book into 2 parts. For starters, it would have been a very long book otherwise. More importantly, though, there was some exciting changes in my daughter's life while I was writing book 3.

That said, I deeply appreciate my readers sticking with me through Tatum's saga. Your loyalty and patience don't go unnoticed.

Choices last a moment. Consequences last a lifetime.

Make sure your choices are yours!

Peace,

Suzie T.

AN EXCERPT FROM:
GIRL DEPARTS THREE, PART 2

Suzie T. Roos

CHAPTER 1

Tatum

Friday, June 1, 1990

I EXAMINED THE OUTDOORS AS IF I'd been in solitary confinement my whole eighteen years. And after finding out I was nine weeks pregnant instead of four, solitary confinement looked pretty darn good.

Staring mindlessly out Dr. O'Connell's office window, I examined the grounds with their well-manicured and perfectly shaped trees. When I heard the office door squeak open, I didn't want to turn away from the view. Didn't want to face Zach.

I took a deep breath, held it, and turned. Zach and Dr. O'Connell stood there with sickening smiles on their faces.

Lord, give me strength.

Zach looked happier than I'd ever seen him.

"Tatum, I was just talking to Zach out in the hall . . . he insisted on paying for all of your medical expenses. Now we have that out of the way, why don't we talk about your baby?"

Oh Jesus. I rubbed the back of my neck, swiping off

the dampness.

Zach sat next to me and took my hand.

I forced a smile. He had no idea what was going on inside me. Not a clue. I loved him so much, but this would destroy him.

Dr. O'Connell took a seat in his plush leather chair and leaned into the desk. "So, your due date is December twenty-fifth."

"Oh, Jesus," I mumbled. Once Zach did the math, he would realize he wasn't the father. I couldn't look at him.

He shifted in his seat and grabbed my shoulders. "Oh my god, Tate. We're having a Christmas baby. Wait 'til Mom hears." He pulled me in all the way for a bear hug.

"Don't thank me, Zach." He let me back down in my seat. The one time I needed him to figure something out on his own and he didn't. The doctor's office was not the place to tell him that he wasn't the biological father of my child. "I can go early. My mom never carried to her due dates. It's just a rough estimate. Right, Doctor?"

"That's right. Zach, she's not far along. Tatum is small, and she may not carry to full term. When she was born, she barely weighed five pounds."

"Really?"

Zach's starstruck eyes made me feel even worse. I sucked in another deep breath with a smile. "That's what they tell me."

"In our family, we have big babies. I was nine pounds and twenty-three inches long. So what are the odds for our baby?"

"Well, Zach . . ." Dr. O'Connell glanced down at

my paperwork, writing notes. "Safe to say somewhere in between there." He glanced up and grinned.

I had to get out of there. Needed fresh air. Needed air, period, to breathe.

"That's about it for now. If there are no more questions, I'll see you two next month, and we can do another ultrasound. Tatum, take your prenatal vitamins like we discussed, and make your appointment for four weeks. You two stay strong, and you'll be okay. Teenage pregnancy isn't easy, but if I know Tatum, you'll be fine."

Zach smiled and brought my hand up to his lips for a soft, enduring kiss. How I hated myself right now.

After we got a stack of papers thicker than the Oxford dictionary and made the next appointment, we were on our way home to the Manor—Tyler's house. A Bertano family gathering was the last thing I wanted. Zach and I needed to be alone for what I was about to tell him. He needed to know now, before we got back to his family's house.

Even though it was early in the summer, the St. Louis humidity was not helping my swelling. "Zach, can you turn up the air? Is it even working?" I swiped the sweat beads off my hairline.

Zach turned the blower up and kept one hand on the steering wheel. After cool air was blowing in my face, he put his hand on my knee.

"Mom will love the idea of a Christmas baby. If you only knew how happy you're going to make my family. Honey—"

"The baby isn't yours," I blurted, unable to keep the secret any longer. I let out a breath of relief. But then seeing Zach's shattered heart written across his face made any relief evaporate. The eerie silence in the car hummed in my ears.

Zach watched the road, but life left his face. "What did you just say?"

If only my heart would give me a few more beats to get this out before it stopped completely. "Zach, I'm so sorry." The weight on my chest dropped to my stomach and rebounded up to my head. I couldn't take much more.

"Zach, I'm nine weeks pregnant. Not four. Do the math. Women carry a baby for forty weeks." One blink and tears violently rolled down my face. Telling him he wasn't the biological father was harder than telling my mom I was pregnant had been. I would never forgive myself for hurting him like this. He deserved better. "I want you to know, I love you so much, but I can't take your money. Your help. Your anything. This child is not your responsibility, Zach. It's Nigel's and mine."

He pulled over and slammed the car into Park. "You think for one minute I won't be there?" He faced the front again and cupped the palm of his hand on the steering wheel. "So the baby is Nigel's? The guy who cheated on you? The guy who was never honest with you?" Zach whipped his stare at me.

Cars were speeding past, inches away from Zach's car sitting on the side of the road, which made me nervous.

He was giving me that look, the look that said, *You don't believe what you're saying, so don't expect me to believe it.* I knew Zach would not turn away from me and the baby, his biological child or not. That wasn't the kind of guy Zach was. My heart slowed. I didn't know what to say. Asking Zach to raise Nigel's child felt wrong.

"Don't tell him. Don't tell anyone. I want this child, Tatum. Look . . . you know what this baby means to me and my family. This baby . . ." He pointed to my stomach. "This child of mine is my family's ticket out of Gramps's old Mob world. We all want out. This baby secures a vineyard in Italy. My vineyard. If Mr. Davidae or Gramps finds out this baby is not a Bertano, we're screwed. Not only would I be on the next flight out, I'd have to marry that whore, Mariacella. Oh, no." Zach shook his head. "No. I'm staying with you, and this baby is mine. Nigel can't have you. I won't allow it."

Zach's determination gave me pause, wondering what the conditions were in this deal. "Zach, I have to tell Nigel. How would you feel if the shoe was on the other foot? You would kill me for keeping this child from you. Doesn't Nigel have a right to know this child is his? I hate secrets. We can do whatever you want with your family, but I have to tell Nigel." I pulled the seatbelt so there was slack for me to turn sideways and put my knee on the seat to face him.

"*No.* You do not have to tell him. We can still claim this child is mine. Now . . . you know Nigel and I are different, but . . ." He huffed a chuckle. "We have some similarities. We both have black, wavy hair."

Seeing Zach so desperate made my heart gush. I reached out for his face, stroking his skin. It was softer than satin. "Hon? He's not six feet three. He doesn't have darker skin. He has blue eyes."

"Details. Your dad is tall."

We both looked at each other and knew. We were

screwed. "Maybe this is a sign."

"A sign?"

"We were never supposed to be together." A knife-like pain penetrated my gut and had me holding my stomach.

"That's bullshit. We were made for each other. And you know it." Zach grabbed the side of my head and pulled me up to his lips.

Feeling Zach's skin on mine lifted the weight from my chest—the pain—the regret. I felt my soulmate was showing me how much he loved me. And this baby.

"Oh, Zach . . . what do we do? Your family's waiting on us."

"Shit." Zach rested his forehead on mine. "Well, all hell will break lose if Gramps finds out this child isn't one of us." He met my gaze, then tucked in the bottom of his lip and bit. Thinking.

I couldn't tell him that gesture alone proved Zach was my happy place.

"Gramps won't be there anyway. I'll tell Mom and Dad. Then when the time comes, I'll have Dad tell Gramps. I want to make sure all of the paperwork—the contract and the deed to the vineyard—is in place and in my name before Gramps finds out. Then when he does, I'll deal with him. One thing at a time."

"How can you be so calm? I'm sweating over here. I screwed up my life nine weeks ago, and then I dragged yours down the toilet with mine in one quick office visit."

Zach grinned and ran his hand down the side of my head. "It took you longer than an office visit! Besides, you didn't screw up my life, nor did you wreck yours. If this is what we have to do to be together, so be it. I'm calm because you've told me you love me. And the best part is, you haven't said you're leaving me. Everything else . . . I can deal with."

Zach was more than understanding. I always said he wasn't a normal guy, and he wasn't. A "normal" guy would have run for the hills, never looking back. I realized how lucky I was—I was a screw-up from a middle-class family nothing to my name but a Sak purse filled with cheap lip balm, a picture of my grandma, and old mascara. I didn't deserve a guy who supported and loved me no matter how much I complicated our lives. The happy cry came running to the forefront. My emotions were all over the spectrum.

"Oh, Zach, I wish things were different. Because you make it so easy to love you."

Zach got back in the driver's seat and drove off with a mischievous grin. "If we weren't in public and on a main road, I'd pull your ass in that back seat with me. Because you make it easy for me to love you too."

The impulse to touch him won, and I placed my hand on his knee and slowly moved up his leg. "If only we were older."

"Older? What does that have to do with anything?" He laughed.

I rubbed his thigh. "We'd tell certain people to screw off and then we could be together. We wouldn't have to answer to anyone." I turned to him but kept my hand on his leg. "Gramps. My parents. Your ex-fiancée. Everyone who gets in the way of what we want in life needs to screw off."

The corner of Zach's sexy mouth went up. "You're sounding more and more like a Lead Bertano."

Oh no. "Is that how they talk?" I backed up against the car door.

"Exactly. The difference is, they follow through. You can totally be a Bertano, Tatum. If you let yourself."

He pulled into the Manor's driveway. Cars flooded the street. He pulled out his keys, and they rattled in his hand. "You can have everything . . . if you'd take it."

Deep down, we both knew nothing was free, though.

He kissed my lips and ran around to my car door and opened it for me. "Let's do this."

I took his hand and we went inside, together. With Zach by my side, embraced by his love and support, maybe we could conquer anything.

ACKNOWLEDGEMENTS

I can't believe it's been 11 months since I released Girl Spoken For, the first in the Spoken For Series. Putting three books out in less than a year takes a team with a great work ethic, patience and loyalty.

Thanks again for another job well done to Marlo Berliner (Chimera Editing), Amanda Sumner (Careful Copyediting), Dana Waganer and Diana Drake for all of the editing, proofreading, beta reading, critiquing and more!!

Thanks also to Jennifer Jakes for formatting and everything in between to get this book re-released. You are a true friend.

Thanks to K Keeton Designs for creating me bright new beautiful covers (2022). You even read the entire series just to give me new covers that would accurately represent the books. I love the new covers and you.

And thanks to my fellow author friends for your critiquing, brainstorming and friendship. Your willingness to help me succeed is very much appreciated and invaluable. Michelle Sharp, Diana Drake, Jennifer Jakes, Claudia Shelton & Linda Gilman. Thank you!

Last, but not least, thanks to my family. You three are the absolute best, I love you, G-V-J!

ABOUT THE AUTHOR

Suzie T. Roos is from, and has settled in, St. Louis with her husband, two grown children, a bossy little Wesite mix and a lazy Turkish Angora kitty. As of fall 2016, she has a son-in-law. Which has led to her first grandbaby arriving spring of 2022.

Suzie and her husband were high school sweethearts and during that time she got pregnant with their daughter. Years later, their adventures took them to a few different residents from Philadelphia, PA to out West in Santa Monica, Ca. They're thankful they could expose their children to different American lifestyles and cultures.

Suzie has self-published four YA novels—Girl Spoken For, Girl Divided Two, Girl Departs Three (Part 1 & Part 2).

Besides writing, Suzie's hobbies include movies, traveling, and especially concert going with her husband and friends.

She's always been an animal lover and animal rights advocate. She is certified by FEMA in IS-00011.a Animal in Disasters: Community Planning. She's also an active volunteer at the Humane Society of Missouri.

www.suzietroos.com
www.facebook.com/SuzieT.Roos
twitter.com/@suzietroosbooks

ALSO BY SUZIE T. ROOS

www.ingramcontent.com/pod-product-compliance
Lightning Source LLC
Chambersburg PA
CBHW051426170626
46809CB00006B/2334